Miss Switch
online

Also by
Barbara Brooks Wallace

Peppermints in the Parlor
The Barrel in the Basement
The Twin in the Tavern
Cousins in the Castle
Sparrows in the Scullery
Ghosts in the Gallery
Secret in St. Something
The Perils of Peppermints

The Trouble with Miss Switch
Miss Switch to the Rescue

Miss Switch
online

Barbara Brooks Wallace

ALADDIN PAPERBACKS
New York   London   Toronto   Sydney   Singapore

First Aladdin Paperbacks edition December 2003

Copyright © 2002 by Barbara Brooks Wallace

ALADDIN PAPERBACKS
An imprint of Simon & Schuster Children's Publishing Division
1230 Avenue of the Americas
New York, NY 10020

Also available in an Atheneum Books for Young Readers hardcover edition.
Design by Ann Sullivan
The text of this book was set in Berkeley Oldstyle ITC.

Printed in the United States of America
2 4 6 8 10 9 7 5 3 1

The Library of Congress has cataloged the hardcover edition as follows:
Wallace, Barbara Brooks, 1922–
Miss Switch online / by Barbara Brooks Wallace.
p.   cm.
Sequel to: Miss Switch to the rescue.
Summary: Miss Switch the witch returns to save Rupert and the entire sixth
grade from the evil Saturna, who is operating a sinister Web site and has
installed her brother as principal of the school.
ISBN 0-689-84376-3 (hc)
[1. Witches—Fiction. 2. Schools—Fiction. 3. Computers—Fiction.] I. Title.
PZ7.W1547 Mf 2002
[Fic]—dc21   00-063987
ISBN 0-689-86028-5 (Aladdin pbk.)

To Bizzy and Boo
(you know who you are)
with lots of love
and a couple of genuine magic spells, too

ACKNOWLEDGMENTS

To Piper,
without whose inspiration as a bird
of many talents and interests, and as an
accomplished shoulder rider, there might
never have been a Fred in this book.

CONTENTS

Miss Switch
online

1

Profound Thoughts
from the Monkey Bars

Nothing *appeared* to happen on the day I began sixth grade at Pepperdine Elementary School that pointed to the extraordinary, and I have to add *dangerous*, events about to take place in my life. It's as amazing that I'm still here to record them as it was for me to be around to record two similar events that happened earlier. Some of you may choose not to believe what I'm writing on these pages. But as a great and dedicated scientist, which I became in the summer following my year in the fourth grade, I feel I must make this report. I'll be as accurate and truthful as I know how.

The only noticeably different thing about the beginning of this first day of school from every other was the new sixth-grade cool-guy greetings my friends and I exchanged as I sauntered up to where they all sat hunched over on top of the monkey bars of the Pepperdine playground.

"Hey, it's the Broomster! Yay! Yay! Yay!"

The Broomster—that was me, Rupert P. Brown III, also known as Broomstick.

"Hey, it's the Peatmeister! Hey, it's the Creamer! Hey, it's the Bananapeeler! Yay! Yay! Yay!" I said right back, losing no time in joining them.

Peatmeister, of course, was Peatmouse, otherwise Wayne Partlow. Creamer was Creampuff, otherwise Tommy Conrad. Bananapeeler was plain Banana, otherwise Harvey Robert Fanna. Now, once we'd gotten all this cool-guy stuff over with, we'd go back to being good old Peatmouse, Creampuff, Banana, and Broomstick, which we'd called each other since about the third grade. I was just as long and skinny then as I am now, which is how I got my name. But who could have known back there in the third grade how prophetic that nickname would turn out to be!

"Where's the Spookster?" Peatmouse asked as soon as I'd settled myself down beside them all on the top rung.

"She left," I replied. "Her father got transferred. She's about a thousand miles away from here now."

"That's too bad," said Creampuff.

"Yeah," I said, and let it go at that. I didn't see any point in going into how "too bad" it was.

Spookster was Spook, otherwise Amelia Matilda Daley. I'm the one who gave her the name Spook in the fifth grade because of the way she always breathed, "Boy, that's spooky!" when she looked into a microscope. As you may gather, Spook is a fellow scientist as well as a friend. She is the only one who knows the true details of the two earlier events I've mentioned. In order for you to have a better understanding of the report I'm about to make, I'll reveal the most important of those details here.

In the first of the two events, I was introduced to a real, honest-to-goodness, card-carrying witch, Miss Switch. She arrived at Pepperdine Elementary School as our fifth-grade teacher, seeking the help of my great scientific brain to suggest some original witchcraft ideas that would satisfy the command of a goofy contraption called a computowitch. It belonged to a really nasty brand of witch named Saturna. Luckily, I came up with the idea of feeding it the information about what a great teacher Miss Switch was. The computowitch got so excited it practically blew itself up, and thus we got rid of Saturna. Or so I thought.

But back she came, now determined to get rid of the one who had put her computowitch out of commission. That, of course, was me. Saturna tried to have me kidnapped, but it was Amelia who got kidnapped instead. Fortunately, Miss Switch came to the rescue. After some pretty scary events, all ended up well, and once again we got rid of Saturna. Or so I thought!

At any rate, I now return to the conversation I was having with my friends on the top rung of the Pepperdine monkey bars. After the greetings were over with, the first topic of conversation, as it always had been, was noteworthy events of that summer. My contribution was that I got another pet, a cockatiel, named Fred. I said "another" because he was in addition to my turtle, Caruso, and my two guinea pigs, Hector and Guinevere. Fred was a consolation prize from my parents because I didn't get to go to camp that summer. They had finally decided that camp was a waste of my time and their money, which I'd been telling them all along. But if they wanted to console me with Fred, I was not going to argue.

After all this we were ready for the burning question of who our teacher was going to be that year.

"Maybe we'll just get Mrs. Fitzgerald again," Peatmouse said.

"She's okay," Creampuff said. "We liked her most of the time."

"Yeah," we all agreed.

"You know what the real problem is, don't you?" I said. "It's not Mrs. Fitzgerald. It's just that once you've had the best, nothing else is ever going to seem that good."

It took them all zero seconds to know exactly the person I was talking about.

"Miss Switch!" Peatmouse said.

"Yeah!" said Banana and Creampuff.

"And the thing is," said Peatmouse, "that we could never really explain why we were so nutty about her."

"The whole class was," said Creampuff. "But looking at her, you'd think we were all just plain nutty."

I couldn't argue with that one. I now refer you to some notes I made once regarding her looks:

a. Sharp nose that could crack granite.

b. Ridiculous little old-fashioned wire spectacles (resting on said nose) that instantly stop looking ridiculous when her eyes are drilling holes into some poor fifth-grade victim.

c. Chin that could substitute for a pickax.

d. Black hair rolled into a bun that looks as if it could not be dislodged with a sledgehammer.

e. Ancient, musty gray dress that could have been rescued from somebody's old attic trunk.

f. General appearance as cuddly as a steel knitting needle.

"She was strict, too," said Banana. "Boy, was she strict! I mean, on a 'strict' scale of one to ten, try fifteen."

"Then why did we like her so much?" asked Peatmouse. "I mean besides her being the best teacher we've ever had?"

We all looked at one another and said it at the same time: "Because she was so *fair!*"

And that was probably the biggest reason. She wasn't just the best teacher, but the *fairest* we'd ever had. When she had something unpleasant to say to you regarding your behavior in class, or your latest rotten English or arithmetic paper, and you watched her nose growing sharper, and felt her eyes turning your blood to ice, and you wondered if your life was about to end right there and then as her pickax chin chopped you to pieces, you always knew one thing: that you'd earned it!

"On a 'fair' scale of one to ten, you'd have to pick a number so long, it fell off the blackboard," said Banana.

"Off the world," said Creampuff.

"Out of the universe," said Peatmouse.

"Yeah!" I said.

"Does anyone think she might be back?" Banana asked.

"Not a chance," I said.

"Why not, Broomstick?" asked Creampuff.

"That's just my opinion," I said.

Anyway, how could I tell them exactly "why not"? Spook was the only one I could discuss that with. After all, as I said, she was the only one who knew who Miss Switch *really* was, and that she would probably be back here only if trouble were brewing.

As far as I could see, there was nothing in sight by way of trouble that could possibly need Miss Switch's special talents. Therefore, we could not expect her to appear in the sixth-grade classroom.

But then how was I to know my opinion was wrong? Dead wrong. For that very night when I sat down at my computer to e-mail Spook at spook@home.com, something sinister was already developing that was aimed right at me, Rupert P. Brown III. And not only at me, but also at Peatmouse, Banana, Creampuff, and the whole Pepperdine Elementary School sixth grade!

2

Suffering from Swooning

I don't know what further discussions we might have had about Miss Switch if the school bell hadn't rung. We all scrambled down from the monkey bars and headed across the blacktop toward the building. It was then a thought struck me. "Banana," I said, "isn't your mother some kind of a big wheel in the PTA?"

"Yeah," said Banana, looking uncomfortable. "President. Why?"

"I'd think *she'd* know who our teacher is," I said. "Didn't she tell you?"

"No," said Banana. "If she did, wouldn't I have said? I think she knows, but she says unless it's a matter of life or death, I'm going to have to find things out just like everyone else whose mother is not PTA president."

We all shrugged. There went the pipeline to interesting advance information.

"I did find out something, though," Banana said quickly, as if he needed to make up for his mother's unfortunate attitude. "I heard her talking to someone on the telephone about it. Mrs. Grimble had an accident and busted an arm and a leg. There's going to be a substitute principal until she gets back."

Substitute? Wasn't that what Miss Switch had been, a substitute? So what if it was as a substitute *teacher*? Wasn't it just possible she could just as well come as a substitute *principal*? I was having difficulty breathing thinking about it.

"Did you hear any name . . . er . . . *mentioned*, Banana?" I asked, digging for clues.

"No," said Banana, "but my mother was giggling, and her face was all pink."

"She must have changed the subject. I never heard of anyone giggling about a new principal," said Peatmouse.

You couldn't argue with that. Anyway, first things first, and we were now about to find out who was going to be leading us through the perils of sixth grade. Hands in pockets, being cool-guy sixth graders, we slouched on down the old, familiar Pepperdine hallway, and entered the door of Room Twelve.

Oh, no!

Seated at the teacher's desk was not our fifth-grade teacher, Mrs. Fitzgerald. Instead it was very old Mrs. Potts, who had been our teacher in *second* grade! I thought she had retired the year before. Was she going to be able to remember that second grade had been replaced with sixth grade?

She beamed at us as we all filed into the room.

"My!" she said. "Almost all of my old second-grade class back with me again. Isn't it wonderful? Why, there's Rupert, and Wayne, and Tommy, and Harvey. Oh, and there's Melvin and Billy and . . . and oh, so many of you."

We smiled weakly at Mrs. Potts, found desks for ourselves, and fell into them. I didn't mind about everyone else, but I couldn't agree with Mrs. Potts about Melvin Bothwick and Billy Swanson being wonderful in anyone's class. Melvin was a sneak and a tattletale, and Billy was an oversized bully who thought he could get away with just about anything. He had made every teacher's life miserable, including Mrs. Potts, since the first grade. If she couldn't remember, how was she going to remember we weren't her little second graders anymore?

The bell rang, and the school year officially began. But you wouldn't have known it from the hubbub continuing in the classroom.

"Now, children, children!" Mrs. Potts said helplessly.

But the boys kept on shoving and punching each other in the ribs as books were passed out. The girls kept on talking to each other. And Billy Swanson was already at work tearing off bits of paper and making the spitballs for which he had been famous all through first, second, third, fourth, and fifth grade. I could see that things were not looking good for the sixth grade.

Would this situation in Miss Switch's former fifth grade be enough to bring her back as our substitute principal? How long was I going to have to wait to find out? As it turned out, no more than an hour later Mrs. Potts made the following announcement:

"The new principal will be visiting each class this morning, starting with our class. Why, it should be about this very minute!" Sure enough, at that moment, voices were heard approaching Room Twelve. My eyes were nailed to the doorway. Soon all would be revealed.

First through the door came Mrs. Fanna, Banana's mother, president of the PTA. Now, I could understand why a mother who is president of the PTA might have to dress up a little to take the principal on a tour of the school. But Mrs. Fanna, who generally appeared at Pepperdine like most of the other mothers in whatever baggy old clothes she could find in her closet, was so dressed up it was ridiculous. Her cheeks were flushed, and she had a goofy smile on her face.

Right behind Mrs. Fanna appeared a small woman approximately the shape of a rain barrel and not much taller. Her face, as round as a full moon, exactly matched the rest of her. She only looked at the class briefly, however, as she came through the door, because she was too busy trying to balance an enormous green notebook in one hand and scratch notes in it with the other.

Right behind her someone else came striding in. And my high hopes came crashing down. It was not Miss Switch. It was not Miss Anything. It was not even Mrs. Anything. It was *Mr.* Something! But this was not just *any* Mr. Something. This was the handsomest man I'd ever seen in my life!

What I mean is, that on a scale of one to ten—oh well, forget it. I couldn't come up with a scale long enough. All I can say is you had to be there to see the moony looks develop on the faces of every girl in the class as soon as they saw him. The same look even appeared on the face of old Mrs. Potts, not to mention the moony look on the moon-faced person whose pen began skittering all over her notebook as she gazed up at this fellow. As for Mrs. Fanna, she was so busy fluttering her eyelashes at him that for a few moments it seemed as if she had forgotten what the president of the PTA was supposed to be doing in front of the sixth-grade class. Banana slunk down into his desk, looking as if he would like to slide under it and never be seen again.

But Mrs. Fanna finally managed to stop fluttering long enough to let us know that this was our acting principal, Mr. Dorking, and his assistant, Miss Tuna. Then Mrs. Fanna got even more flustered, and started clapping. I couldn't see why this event called for applause, but like a bunch of sixth-grade sheep, we all clapped away.

After that, Mr. Dorking made a speech of about two sentences. He told us how happy he was to be at Pepperdine Elementary School. He told us how happy he was to be talking to the sixth grade. And while he was telling us these exciting things, the girls were all swooning at their desks. Mrs. Potts, Mrs. Fanna, and Miss Tuna were likewise swooning. When Mr. Dorking had finished inspiring the sixth grade with his speech, he flashed us a gazillion-dollar smile and left the room with Mrs. Fanna and

Miss Tuna practically fainting behind him. Banana finally slithered back up in his desk seat, trying to look as if he had no connection whatsoever to the whole event.

The day didn't get any better. Billy Swanson built up a big arsenal of spitballs, and they began whizzing around the room. Mrs. Potts finally gave up and sent him to the principal. That only improved the Billy Swanson situation slightly, but it unfortunately gave the girls ideas. They started giggling and whispering and passing notes so busily that Mrs. Potts gave up on that as well and started sending them in relays to the principal. Which is just what they wanted! They came back looking moonier than ever after seeing Mr. Dorking, and by the end of the day they were calling him Adorable Dorry.

I began to wonder how Mrs. Potts was going to last the day, much less the year. But then I was in for another shock. Just before the closing bell, Mrs. Potts told us how much she had enjoyed having her second-grade class again, and how sorry she was that it was for only one day. Our regular teacher, however, who had been delayed in flight, would be there with us in the morning.

Mrs. Potts only there for a day! A teacher delayed in flight! Flight! The word rang in my ears. Who was there to say it had to be by airplane? Could it mean—could it mean—*another* form of air transport? I hardly allowed myself to think the word. No, I told myself, stop thinking this has anything to do with Miss Switch. There is no more reason for her to come back now than there had been. Forget it! Forget Miss Switch!

3

❂   ❂   ❂   ❂   ❂   ❂   ❂

COMPUTOWITCH.COM

❂   ❂   ❂   ❂   ❂   ❂   ❂

I finally got to my computer late that night. My parents had already gone to bed. So except for an occasional tiny splash from Caruso climbing off his rock into his pool, or Hector and Guinevere taking a spin on their respective wheels, the house was silent. Except for the small light over my desk, my room was also dark. There was just me, with Fred perched on my shoulder, where he always is when I'm in my room, sitting there in a small pool of light.

❂   ❂   ❂

TO: spook@home.com
FROM: broomstick@home.com
SUBJECT: A very weird day

Hi! Thanks for your letter. I'm glad your
parents decided not to buy a house after all.
Maybe your father thinks he's going to be sent
back here. I told you I'd be looking for a crazy
magic toadstool, **toadstoolius spookus returnicum**, but you and I both know I wouldn't know
one if I found one, or how to use it. I'd have
to have Miss Switch here for that. And no, as
you could probably guess, she wasn't at school
this morning. But it was a very weird day.

   Our teacher was Mrs. Potts. Remember her from
the second grade? Billy Swanson did his usual
and sent off about twenty spitballs. He got sent
to the principal, and so did a bunch of the
girls, but they were **trying** to get sent. Which
brings me to the real reason why the day was so
weird.

   Mrs. Grimble had an accident and broke a leg
and an arm, so she's gone for a while. We now have
a substitute principal. It's a man named Mr.
Dorking, and he is the best-looking guy I have ever
seen in my life. I'm not kidding you, Spook. The
girls were all swooning. Even Mrs. Potts swooned.

Anyway, at the end of the day, Mrs. Potts announced she was only there for that day, which was probably a good thing because I didn't think she could make it through another one. She said she was filling in for our regular teacher, who had been "delayed in flight"—her exact words.

I know you're thinking the same thing I did: flight! Miss Switch! But there are two problems with concluding anything from this, as I see it.

a. Good as she is at her particular means of air travel, I don't see how she could be delayed by anything.

b. Nothing scary happened today that would bring her running, or in her case, flying. A principal who has all the girls swooning over him is pretty disgusting, but it isn't exactly a dangerous situation.

Of course there's always the possibility that Miss Switch needs help herself, like the first time she came seeking the help of my great scientific brain. I still find it hard to believe that Miss Switch was being ordered around by a crazy contraption that was nothing but a dinky, black, old-fashioned cooking stove. Someone had a lot of nerve giving it that scientific name: computowitch!

And that word turned out to be the last one in my letter. As soon as I had entered it, my computer screen instantly turned a sickly green, as if it were about to—well—throw up. Then it started to shiver. My first thought was that I'd hit the wrong key, although I'd never known of any key on the keyboard that produced these results before.

My second thought was that my computer might be about to crash and take the letter I'd spent all my valuable time writing right along with it! I wasn't about to let that happen. Swiftly, I somehow managed to grab the mouse and shoot the arrow on the screen up to hit "send." Gone! I'd saved the letter. It was on its way to Spook.

All except that one word—"computowitch." It remained on the screen, quivering in the sea of pea-soup green. I practically stopped breathing. So that was it! I hadn't hit the wrong key. There probably wasn't even any wrong key to hit. It was the word "computowitch." I continued to stare at the screen, hypnotized, wondering what was going to happen next. I didn't have to wait long.

The screen turned a fiery, feverish red. Then it changed to orange, then purple, and then back to red again. Meanwhile, the computer began heaving in and out, looking as if it were ready to explode. It must have scared Fred, because he catapulted from my shoulder and flew over to huddle in his cage.

I suddenly realized my computer was behaving almost the same as that crazy computowitch had just before it died! Is that what my computer was about to do? Almost automatically, my hand shot out and pulled the plug from the wall. The screen instantly went dark. But was the computer still working? Hesitantly, I shoved the plug back in, and the screen turned the good old familiar cool blue. It was apparently back in business!

But how had all that wacky stuff happened? How could just the single word "computowitch" have caused it? Unless it had some connection with the original computowitch, the one that I, personally, had been responsible for wrecking. The last I knew, it was going back to be used as a plain old stove. There was certainly something very odd about all of it. Maybe even something sinister.

And then I thought of the letter I had just sent off to Spook. The word "computowitch" had apparently never gone off with the rest of it. But what if Spook used the word when she replied? Hadn't I better warn her about it?

TO: spook@home.com
FROM: broomstick@home.com

subject: PS to earlier message—IMPORTANT!

This has to do with the letter I just sent you. I mentioned a certain item at the end, but if you write back about it, please don't use the "c" word for it. Maybe you'd better not mention it at all. Something strange is happening. I don't know what it is, but until I find out, we have to play it safe. So please remember, spook, no "c" word!

Broomstick

I sent the letter off at once but went right on sitting there staring at the blank screen. "I don't know what it is, but until I find out . . ." I had written. Find out what? But more to the point, *how?* Where did it all begin? I didn't really think science was going to come to my rescue. I mean, what could I do with a test tube, beaker, or a Bunsen burner in a case like this?

The only thing I *could* think of to do was too dangerous. After all, I'd warned Spook about it. And yet, even as I was thinking this, I knew I *was* going to do it. I took a deep breath, clenched my jaw, and entered the word "computowitch." I knew I was taking a terrible risk, but only hoped that if I blew up my room, and possibly myself along with it, my parents would understand.

Holding my breath, I watched the exact same thing happen as before! The screen turned pea-soup green and started to shiver. It then turned the same fierce red again. In the meantime, the computer was repeating its act of heaving ferociously in and out. I was scared, and getting more scared every second. At last I couldn't stand it anymore, and I gave myself a command decision to reach for the plug. But before my fingers had arrived at their destination, my computer gave one final shuddering heave and stopped cold.

I wasn't convinced it was finished, however, so I kept my hand near the plug just in case. After all, the screen was still shivering. But then the colors instantly began to reverse themselves. The red turned back to purple, then orange, then red again, and finally back to pea soup green. Then the screen stopped shivering, and all that remained of this whole act was the word "computowitch" sitting there.

I have to admit, this was a big letdown. It was not that I liked the idea of my parents having to come in and gather up some pieces of me and my room if something disastrous had happened. But I had let myself get scared out of my wits, and practically stopped a kind of experiment where I might have been on the brink of making some huge discovery. And now it had all ended up with just me just sitting and staring at the screen with the word "computowitch" on it doing absolutely nothing.

Somehow, I couldn't tear myself away. I just sat

there. Then something curious happened. I felt a strange tingling feeling in my fingers. Then they began to twitch. A moment later, I watched them float up off my lap and settle on the keyboard. It was as if I were watching someone else put their fingers on the keys. Then, right next to "computowitch," these fingers typed in ".com." Instantly, on the lower left side of the screen appeared a box that read, "Enter password." I'd bumped right into a *very interesting* Web site—computowitch.com! My heart began to race.

Still, what use was a Web site if I didn't know the password? But then my great scientific reasoning powers went to work. What one word could I connect with the old computowitch that would make a good password? How about the name of a person who had suggested the grand idea of having a piece of junk issuing orders to everyone in the first place? I might be wrong. I might even be dangerously wrong typing it in. But I'd come this far, and I wasn't going to back off now. "Here goes!" I told myself, and looking around my familiar room for maybe the last time, I typed "SATURNA."

Wham!

Bang!

I'd got it! And I was still sitting there all in one piece as the message appeared on the screen. Around the border of the page was a mysterious design of curled and pointed lines laced with stars and moons. But what I immediately zeroed in on was the message in the middle of the screen:

"Oh, burning sun
It has begun,
Oh, icy moon
It's none too soon,
We must not fail
To end their tale."

What has begun? I felt prickles running down my back. This was ominous. I was now convinced that something very scary was going on. I waited for something else to appear on the screen. At last I realized that nothing more was going to be revealed, so I shut down the computer and dragged myself off to bed, my mind still spinning.

Could all this possibly have anything to do with Miss Switch? Could it be that I'd walk into the sixth-grade classroom in the morning and find her sitting there at the teacher's desk?

Of course, if Miss Switch were back, it would have to be because she was in terrible trouble. Or someone else was. And I had the unpleasant feeling that it was I, Rupert P. Brown III, who had been selected for that privilege!

4

۞ ۞ ۞ ۞ ۞ ۞ ۞

Miss Blossom

۞ ۞ ۞ ۞ ۞ ۞ ۞

It was all I could do the next morning not to go racing up to the monkey bars on the Pepperdine playground and report to Peatmouse, Creampuff, and Banana my conclusions that our new teacher might actually end up being Miss Switch. But I'd have to give them my reasons. They'd naturally think I'd gone sailing right off the deep end. I would have to contain my excitement.

When we all strolled into Room Twelve, the new teacher was at her desk. A few other sixth graders had arrived ahead of us and were all at their desks staring at her with their eyes popping, as if somebody had come up from behind them and yelled, "Boo!" The teacher turned and gave us a big toothy smile as we came in. All four of our jaws dropped.

The teacher was not Miss Switch. She was not Mrs. Fitzgerald, either. She was not even very old Mrs. Potts. She was definitely not anyone I had ever seen before, and definitely not even *like* anyone I had ever seen before, especially at Pepperdine Elementary School.

She had this huge mountain of seriously yellow hair piled on top of her head in a circle as big as a sausage, and mile-long eyelashes that looked like they had been borrowed from a pair of centipedes. As for her mouth, it was so big and red my first thought was that she must have been stung by a bunch of bees. Not only that, you could hardly see her dress for all the frills and the lace and bows all over it. It was pink, and to be honest looked like somebody's really old party dress they'd put out for a yard sale. And to top it all off, this teacher's name, written in curly letters on the blackboard, was—Miss Blossom. Miss Blossom? Help! Peatmouse, Banana, Creampuff, and yours truly all smiled weakly at Miss Blossom, staggered over to our desks, and collapsed into them.

Now, no one has to tell me looks aren't everything. Take Miss Switch, for example. So I felt we were going to have to give Miss Blossom a chance. I had to hand it to her. She must have been studying the seating chart, because she knew our names right away. But the first thing she did wasn't too promising.

"Billy," she said, addressing Billy Swanson in what I can only describe as a high, chirpy voice. "Your desk is entirely too small for you. I think you should move to the large one that no one seems to be occupying. I think you'll be much more comfortable in that one, dear."

Billy, of course, had carefully chosen for himself the desk most strategically placed for his spitball-shooting operation. We all knew he wouldn't want to move. On the other hand, nobody had ever worried about if he was comfortable or not in his desk, and no one had ever called him "dear" as far back as any of us could remember. This had its effect. His face pinker than Miss Blossom's dress, he hoisted himself up and shuffled over to the appointed desk.

So far, so good. Except that Melvin Bothwick's hand instantly shot up into the air. "Billy is big as he is because he failed kindergarten," announced Melvin with the usual smug look on his face.

"Now, now, Melvin," said Miss Blossom. "If we have something really important to say about others, we must come up and tell me privately. But it isn't nice to tattletale. I'm certain you have not made Billy happy by what you just said."

No, indeed, Melvin had not made Billy happy. And Billy displayed his unhappiness by blowing several fresh, well-chewed spitballs in Melvin's direction

"Ouch! Ouch! Ouch! Miss Blossom, Billy is blowing spitballs at me," Melvin whined.

Miss Blossom shook her head at him. "Melvin, didn't we agree that it isn't nice to tattletale?"

Melvin sat there glowering, because he hadn't agreed to any such thing.

But Miss Blossom rolled on. "I'm sure Billy didn't mean to blow spitballs at you, and won't do it again, will you, Billy?"

"Oh, no!" Billy said with the kind of grin on his face that the class was all too familiar with. We knew more spitballs would be flying before you could say the word "spit."

I couldn't help thinking how Miss Switch had handled Melvin when he had taken pleasure in revealing to the whole class that my middle name was Peevely. She had made him write "My name is Melvin Tattletale Bothwick" one hundred times in front of everyone.

As the day progressed, it was clear that keeping the class in line was not Miss Blossom's strong point.

The spitballs were whizzing around the room. Some of the other boys started blowing spitballs as well. I have to admit I shot off one or two myself. I mean, in self-defense. A couple of the girls joined in, but mostly they were busy snickering, whispering, and passing notes. I had no doubt they were hoping to get sent back to see Adorable Dorry.

But that never happened. Nobody got sent. All Miss Blossom did was bat her centipede-leg eyelashes and smile sweetly at us. At that moment, I was ready to welcome Mrs. Potts back with open arms.

"What a mess!" Peatmouse observed as we were leaving that afternoon.

"Yeah!" we all agreed.

"Are you sure Miss Switch isn't coming back, Broomstick?" Banana asked. For some reason I was always considered the Miss Switch expert. Actually I was more of an expert than any of them knew, but as I've said, I could never reveal why.

"I'm sure," I said. And I was getting surer all the time. After all, as I wrote Spook, the girls swooning over Mr. Dorking could hardly be considered a dangerous situation, and I didn't think Miss Blossom—hair, eyelashes, mouth, and all—could be, either. As for what had happened with my computer, that message on computowitch.com could have been meant for anyone. I just happened to be the one to bump into it.

"Well, it's going to be a mess, anyway," said Peatmouse.

"Yeah!" we all agreed.

5

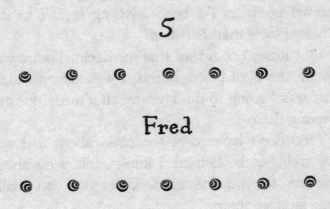

Fred

"That's not where the decimal point goes!"

"Sure it is," I said.

I was sitting at my desk doing my math homework. How Miss Blossom had managed to give us homework, or teach us anything at all, was a surprise to me, things being as they were. But it had been such a loony day, I was ending up actually talking to myself. And, I might add, answering myself as well.

"No, it isn't!" I heard myself insist. "Try moving it over two places and see what happens. You're going to come out with a ridiculous answer if you don't. Go ahead, why not try it?"

"Oh, all right," I said, and grudgingly moved the decimal point as I'd been advising myself to do. "There, how's that? Satisfied?"

Of course, I could see that the decimal point was now in the right place, but as it was my own idea, what was I going to do, give myself a medal for discovering that?

"You don't have to be so snarky about it. I was only trying to be helpful. I know quite a bit about numbers, for your information. I'm glad you finally came around, matey."

"Of course I came around," I grumped. "Besides . . ."

I never finished what I was going to say, because at that moment, if I'd been a comic strip character, you would have seen a big bulb light up right over my head. I wasn't talking to myself at all. I was actually having a conversation with someone else. But, who? Who was there besides Fred, sitting on my shoulder, Caruso in his turtle bowl, and Hector and Guinevere in their respective guinea pig cages? And then another light bulb came on. The other voice had been coming from very close to my right ear.

"Fred?"

"What is it, matey?" replied Fred.

"Is it you who's been talking to me?" I asked,

"Of course it was me," Fred said, "or 'I,' if you prefer. I like 'I' myself, being a grammarian of the old school and a bird who . . . oh, I beg your pardon. I seem to have wandered from the subject. But, yes, I'm the one who's been talking to you. Who else could it have been? You didn't think you were having a conversation with yourself, did you?"

"No," I said promptly, going strictly against my truthful scientific nature. But I could hardly admit that that's exactly the stupid thing I was doing to this opinionated bird, pet or no pet. And it was then that yet another bulb lit up over my head. "But it could have been Caruso or Hector or Guinevere," I said, letting this smarty-pants bird figure out for himself who they were.

"*Them?*" Fred said, and guffawed right in my ear. I think it was a guffaw, anyway. At least it's as close as I can get to what a bird would do.

"What do you mean by referring to us as '*them*' in that tone, you . . . you . . . you overbearing collection of feathers," came an outraged voice from across the room. It was the voice of Guinevere. "You don't have to be so high and mighty just because you sit on Rupert's shoulder. We've all been here a lot longer than you have. And don't think we didn't see that disgraceful performance you gave last night. You ought to be ashamed of yourself, flying off to hide in your cage and leaving poor Rupert to face that crazed machine all by himself. You should have your tail feathers clipped!"

"And for your information," Hector broke in, "Guinevere and I once performed a very useful scientific service for Rupert as a nutrition experiment."

"So, what does a turtle do besides sun himself under a lamp all day and take a dip in his own private pool?" Fred said.

"Well, I may have never done much for science," Caruso returned. "But I do provide entertainment to soothe the scientific brain. I'm quite a singer, you may have noticed."

"I hadn't," Fred replied. "Actually, I do some singing myself. But I have other far more useful talents where Rupert is concerned. I don't suppose you noted my helping with his math this evening?"

"Some help," said Caruso, "moving one decimal point! I could do as much riding around on his shoulder looking down on his homework."

"That's a picture!" said Fred. "A turtle riding around on someone's shoulder. How would you propose to do that?"

"I could if someone would build me a nice little basket," said Caruso.

"A turtle riding around in a basket on someone's

shoulder!" hooted Fred. "That's a laugh. You need to have someone look into your head and see what's riding around in *there*."

I don't know what made me sit there listening to all this. Maybe it was just the shock of being able to actually hear my pets talking. But this had gone on long enough.

"See here, all of you," I said sternly. "You're all going to have to get along. Or . . ." I added ominously, "somebody's going to have to go." I waited a few tense moments for this to be digested. "Now, Hector, Guinevere, and Caruso," I continued, "you've had your moments, all three of you, but you get through it and always end up friends, right?"

"Rupert's right. We always do," said Guinevere.

"But, Fred," I said, "you really are going to have to stop being such a pain in the head."

"More like a pain in the tail," Fred said dismally. "I know I can be pretty insufferable at times. I'll try to mend my ways. I'm really sorry. I hope I haven't offended everyone too much. I do apologize."

"There, there, that's quite all right, dear," said Guinevere. "We need to do some apologizing ourselves. After all, just because we've been here longer doesn't give us the right to go lording over anyone. We're glad you're Rupert's new pet, Fred, and we want to be your friends."

"And I'd like to be yours," Fred said, so overcome, he lost his grip on my shoulder and very nearly dropped on top of my math homework.

"Whew!" I said. "I'm glad that's settled. There's something terrifically important we have to discuss. I'm sure it hasn't escaped anyone's notice that here we are talking to each other. I'd like to know what you think is the reason for it."

"Miss Switch!" Guinevere exclaimed.

"My thoughts exactly," I said. "We can talk when Miss Switch is here."

"Oh, Rupert, is she back?" Guinevere asked. "I'm really glad. But on the other hand, doesn't it mean something dreadful has happened?"

"To your first question, she must be," I replied. "But I haven't seen her. And I can't think of anything really terrible that's happened. Well, our new substitute principal is so handsome all the female population of Pepperdine Elementary School is swooning over him. It's pretty sickening, but not dangerous enough to bring Miss Switch running. Then there's our weird new teacher, Miss Blossom. You should see that hair piled on top of her head like a huge lemon ice-cream cone, and those giant eyelashes. And her dress is nothing but a bunch of frills and bows top to bottom."

"The dress sounds rather fetching to me," said Guinevere. "Of course, I'm only a guinea pig, so what do I know about fashion? But have you ever stopped to think, Rupert, that Miss Blossom might be Miss Switch in disguise?"

"Oh, *please!*" I said, throwing a hand to my forehead. Then I added quickly because I didn't want to hurt Guinevere's feelings, "It's a clever idea, but if you ever saw her, you couldn't ask that. Besides, Miss Switch would never put up with the kind of stuff Miss Blossom lets go on right under her nose. The sixth grade is a disaster zone. And another thing, if Miss Blossom were Miss Switch, she'd have given me a sign. She always has."

"Sounds to me like Miss Blossom might not be Miss Switch, but she could just be the reason for Miss Switch being here, if the sixth grade really is a disaster zone," Hector said thoughtfully.

"Maybe," I said. "But I don't think Billy Swanson's spitballs are enough to do it. It's got to be something bigger than that, and I just don't know what. But I think we all agree she's back, only where is she, and who is she?"

There was a sudden flapping of wings in my ear, and Fred drifted down on my desk. "Well," he said, "all I know about this Miss Switch is what I've heard you saying here tonight, and what—and I must apologize for this, Rupert—I've read in your letters to the person you call Spook, but could Miss Switch be someone else in your school? I mean, does she have to be your teacher?"

"Fred's absolutely right, Rupert," said Hector. "Where was it ever written that Miss Switch had to come back as a teacher? She could come back as just about anyone, couldn't she?"

"I guess so," I said doubtfully. "The question is, who? Do you have any other ideas, Fred?"

"Nope. Sorry," replied Fred. "I'm afraid you're on your own. But you did say something about being given a sign. Are you sure no one you bumped into at school today was trying to do that and you missed it because you weren't looking for it? Now, stop and think."

I did. In my mind I ran back over myself in the cafeteria, the library, the playground, and even in the boys' room. Nothing. I couldn't think of anyone who looked promising, much less who'd given me any sign.

"Nobody," I said.

"Well then," said Guinevere, "you'll just have to keep your eyes peeled tomorrow. But I *have* been wondering about something. You don't suppose that . . . that nonsense with your computer might have something to do with Miss Switch, do you?"

Well, wasn't that *exactly* what I'd supposed when it had happened? Miss Blossom appearing at the sixth-grade teacher's desk instead of Miss Switch had driven that idea out of my mind. But Fred had put a new spin on the whole thing. Maybe Miss Switch was not our teacher, but someone else entirely!

"Thanks for reminding me, Guinevere," I said. "I'm going to reenter that Web site now and see what it has to say for itself. You all know what a Web site is, don't you?"

"Oh, for goodness' sake, Rupert," said Guinevere. "I may not be a fashion expert, but I'm not entirely computer illiterate. None of us is after listening to you muttering away at your desk."

"I'll try to stop if you like," I said.

"Oh, please don't!" Hector said. "How else do you think we learn anything?"

"Compute away!" said Caruso.

"Well," I said, "the Web site belongs to Saturna. You probably remember her. This is scary stuff. If the computer is going to put on the same crazy act it did the last time, Fred, you might want to get off my desk and retreat to your cage."

"Not on your life!" Fred exclaimed. "Now I know I'm not going to be ground into bird meat by that machine, I wouldn't miss this for anything."

"Well, okay, then," I replied.

I turned on my computer. Then we all sat in breathless silence while it warmed up. Finally, I typed in "computowitch."

My computer screen did exactly the same thing it did before, but this time I knew better than to touch it. I just sat there feeling old Fred's claws digging a little harder into my shoulder. At last there it was, the word "computowitch." I quickly added the ".com," entered the password "SATURNA," and saw the computowitch.com Web site appear on the screen.

But the poem had been replaced by another one, and I read it aloud to my pets.

> "How very sweet
> Tweet, tweet, tweet, tweet,
> I'll have my chance
> To howl and dance,
> No one's in sight
> Except that fright,
> No you know who
> Is in the brew,
> Bats may squeal
> And vultures wheel,
> But do not fear
> The way is clear."

For moments, this threw everyone in the room

into deep thought. Then Fred broke the silence. "I don't like it," he said. "What's all this 'tweet, tweet, tweet' stuff? Sounds like Saturna's out to get me. What does she have against birds? I ask you."

"I don't think she has a thing against birds, Fred," Guinevere said quickly. "What she does have, it seems to me, is no talent. At least where poetry is concerned. 'Tweet, tweet,' indeed!"

"I certainly agree with that," said Caruso. "But I don't like the sound of some of the other stuff. Howling, and dancing, and bats, and vultures. It makes my shell crawl."

"Well, it certainly doesn't make *me* feel too comfortable," I said. "Especially when you consider she's probably referring to Pepperdine Elementary School, with me in it. But now I think there's more reason to think that what you said earlier about Miss Switch not necessarily coming back as my teacher is dead right. Just think about it. 'No one's in sight/Except that fright.' Who could 'that fright' be but Miss Blossom?"

"Beats us," said Hector.

"But I'll tell you all," I said, "Saturna may be dead right about Miss Blossom not being Miss Switch, but she's dead *wrong* about Miss Switch not knowing what might be going on. After all, look at us, talking to each other. She's got to be here somewhere."

"So, you'll have to keep your eyes peeled tomorrow," said Guinevere. "It's going to turn out all right. I'm sure of it. Only now, Hector, Caruso, and Fred, we'd better tuck ourselves in for the night. Rupert must get his rest."

With that, there was an immediate flapping of wings as Fred flew from my shoulder and ended up perched on the side of Caruso's bowl. "Good night, Caruso!" he said,

"Good night, old fellow," Caruso sang out.

Then Fred flew first to Guinevere's and then to Hector's cage. "Good night, you two!" he said.

"Good night, Fred!" they chorused.

But before Fred went to his cage to put himself to bed as he always did, he flew back and hopped on my shoulder. I felt a tiny peck on my cheek. "Good night, Rupert!" he said.

"Good night, Fred," I said, and reached up to pat his head.

Then he flew off and hopped into his cage.

Moments later, after I turned out the lights, I heard something I hadn't heard in a very long time. It was Caruso's high little voice singing Brahms' "Lullaby." It was a comforting sound, and helped me to remember that I had the support of my pets in whatever might come. But even though I liked to think of myself as a fearless scientist, I really was scared. And I had to admit, I needed all the comfort I could get!

6

A Midnight Expedition

Even with the help of Caruso's lullaby, I didn't think I could ever get to sleep. Thoughts of all that had happened kept going round and round in my head. I finally did drop off, but I didn't know how long I'd been asleep when I awoke with a sudden jolt. I looked at the clock by my bed. It was twelve midnight, right on the dot. I lay in my bed wondering what had awakened me. Then suddenly the picture jumped into my head. The picture became clearer, and my neck began to tingle.

What I was seeing was someone's back. Someone

with black hair in a bun. Someone in a gray dress. Someone in the library! Someone standing with her back to me, nose buried in a book, not moving an inch while I signed out my book at the desk. Just before I turned to leave, the person in the gray dress set her book back on the display shelf where she was standing. *The Sorcery of Science!* All at once I could even picture the very book. *That* must have been Miss Switch, and *that* was the sign! After all, Miss Switch was involved with one thing. I was involved with the other. What could be a clearer sign than that?

I knew almost at once what I had to do. I lay in bed for a few minutes, not moving a muscle, but with my skin creeping as I thought of what lay ahead. Then I slowly threw back my covers.

I decided not to turn on the light because I didn't want to wake the pets and get them all disturbed over what I was about to undertake. But I managed to find my clothes and climb into them. Then I grabbed my mini-flashlight from my bed table and started for the door. Before I'd reached it, however, I heard something come fluttering through the air and land squarely on my shoulder.

"What are you up to, Fred?" I whispered.

"More to the point, what are *you* up to?" he replied.

44

"I just woke up suddenly and remembered some-one I saw who might be Miss Switch," I said. "If it is, this is what she would be expecting me to do."

"Which is?" inquired Fred.

"Meet her at Pepperdine," I said.

"At *midnight*?" Fred gasped.

"That's the usual time for this sort of thing," I replied.

"Well, I'm going with you," Fred said.

"What on earth for?" I asked. "This might turn dangerous."

"Exactly," said Fred. "That's why I'm coming along."

"Look, Fred," I said, "I don't mean to be insulting, but what could someone your size do if I got into trouble?"

"Who knows?" Fred replied. "But I can offer moral support. That's worth something."

I was beginning to get a stiff neck from whispering out of the side of my mouth to Fred, and I had a feeling he'd win out in the end, anyway. So I opened the door, crept out, tiptoed past my parents' room, where they lay peacefully sleeping away, and made it to the front door. Then we set out from the house.

I have to admit it was ridiculously comforting to have Fred along with me, despite his size. There was a moon that night, but dark clouds scudded across it. They cast shadows that danced around us like crazy ghosts. But the worst was when we finally reached the Pepperdine playground. It's one thing to be there in the broad daylight with noisy kids running around and your friends waving to you from the top of the monkey bars. But it's a very different story at night when it's dark and deserted, and silent. Nobody's going down the slides. The swings aren't moving, and the monkey bars sit there like a big bony skeleton.

"Where are we headed?" Fred asked.

"The library," I replied. "It's way at the end of the building. I would guess that's where she'd be, anyway, with her . . . oops!"

"What's that 'oops' mean, Rupert?" Fred asked. "I don't like the sound of it."

"I forgot," I said. "Miss Switch may have her cat Bathsheba with her. She usually does."

"C-C-C-Cat?" quavered Fred, his little beak chattering. "You never mentioned a cat."

"I'm really sorry," I said. "But honestly, I just didn't think of it. Anyway, whose idea was it to come with me—insisted on it, actually?"

"I didn't know there was a c-c-c-cat involved," Fred said. "Your jacket doesn't have a bird-sized pocket in it by any chance, does it?"

"Several that you'd fit right into," I replied. "Are

you ready to go in now? We're just about there."

"I kind of wanted to see this Miss Switch," said Fred. "But maybe I'd better go into hiding until you see who's with her. I can always come out later if it's safe. But could I have an assist, please?"

I reached up, wrapped my fingers around him, and gently stuffed him into one of my pockets. "Do you want to be zipped in?" I asked.

"Not necessary just yet," came the muffled voice from my pocket. "Hey, I really like it in here. Nice and cozy."

"That's good," I said. I missed having him on my shoulder, but I had to respect his feelings about Bathsheba. In his position, my feelings would have been exactly the same.

At any rate, by now we had arrived at what I knew was the library. Its big, dark windows reached all around the end of the building. Its big, *very* dark windows. The reflection from the moon appeared on them, disappeared, then reappeared again as the clouds blew across it. I couldn't help shuddering as I watched them.

"Courage, friend!" came Fred's voice from my pocket.

"Thanks!" I said, my courage being in short supply at that moment.

But I remembered the last time I had seen what

I'd thought was the moon's reflection turned out to be the reflected light of a Bunsen burner inside my classroom, with Miss Switch hovering over it. I had no reason to think there would be a Bunsen burner in the library, but with Miss Switch you never knew. I needed a closer look. Reaching up and grabbing the windowsill, I hoisted myself up onto a ledge that ran around the building, and peered into the window. But except for some dim light from the moon, the library was dark. Pitch-dark. And empty.

"Anything there?" asked the voice in my pocket.

"Nothing that I'm looking for," I replied, and dropped back to the ground. What a letdown! Not that I wanted anything really nasty to happen to Fred and me, but it seemed a real waste of time, getting all scared for nothing. "I guess it's back to school tomorrow with eyes peeled," I said. "Unless . . . unless . . ."

"Unless what?" asked Fred.

"Unless she might be someplace else!" I said excitedly. "And I've got an idea where—my classroom!"

I started to run. Well, it stood to reason, didn't it? Wasn't my classroom where Miss Switch and I had always met before? Of course, that used to be the fifth grade, and now I was in the sixth, but I was certain she would figure that out. I quickly found the

Room Twelve windows, took a deep breath, and hoisted myself up.

"Here goes!" I said, and pressed my nose up against the glass.

And someone was there! Sitting at her desk with a small desk lamp on, marking papers. She must have heard me scrambling onto the ledge, because I had barely pressed my nose against the window, when she looked up. She jumped up and came toward the window. I was so startled, I couldn't even manage a squeak. She unlatched the window and threw it up.

Oh no! It couldn't be, I thought. But it was!

"M-M-M-M-Miss B-B-B-B-Blossom?" I croaked. I very nearly lost my grip on the windowsill and went sailing off the ledge backwards, with Fred and all. "E-E-E-Excuse me, but I was looking for s-s-s-some-one else," I quavered, hoping stupidly that I would not be pressed for details.

"For goodness' sake, Rupert, I *am* someone else," Miss Blossom snapped. "Don't you recognize me? I thought you knew who I was."

"M-M-M-Miss S-S-S-Switch?" I stammered.

"No other," said Miss Blossom. "And you'd better climb on in here before you fall and break your head. It would be a great loss to the scientific community if you did, you know."

I scrambled speedily through the window. But I was still in a daze and had to hang on to the nearest desk to keep from keeling over.

As I was trying to steady myself, I saw Miss Blossom's lips widen into a thin smile. "Didn't recognize me, eh? Splendid!"

Uh-oh! I thought immediately. If this actually was some kind of crazy disguise, couldn't it just as well be disguising Saturna as Miss Switch? Had I walked right into a trap? At any moment, could I find myself turned into a toad or a rat or just about anything? As for poor Fred hiding in my pocket, he could end up birdseed. And what could I do about it? Not much; I'd just have to try to bulldoze my way through, and somehow figure out how to make my escape.

"What's so splendid about it, Miss Switch . . . or Miss Blossom . . . or . . . or . . ."—I paused to narrow my eyes as if I wasn't being fooled for a minute, and was ready to deal with any situation—"or whoever you really are."

"What do you mean by 'whoever you really are'?" asked Miss Blossom, peering out from under her huge eyelashes. "Haven't we just established that?"

"*You* have," I said with the best sneer I could

manage under these conditions. "You . . . you could be just about anybody, for all I know."

"Well, then," said Miss Blossom, "please wipe that silly look off your face, step outside the classroom, close the door behind you, then stand and wait until I call you."

My chance to escape! The school doors were all unlocked on the inside. I could easily get away and race home. Instead, all I did was wipe, step, close, stand like a dumb dodo—and wait.

"What's up?" came the voice from my pocket.

I groaned. "Don't even ask," I said, hoping I wasn't making the biggest mistake of my life.

I couldn't have waited more than three minutes, when the order was given from behind the door: "You may return now, Rupert!"

I did, and was I ever glad I hadn't turned chicken and run off! Standing right where Miss Blossom had stood was a familiar figure all in black—black dress, long black cape, and over long, charcoal-black straight hair, a tall, pointed black hat. From under the brim of the hat, a pair of eyes, slanted and glassy green, shot out sparks that fell hissing onto the teacher's desk. The mountain of lemon-yellow curls was gone. The long eyelashes were gone. The pink dress with the bows and frills was gone.

No, not quite gone. Because those items were all lying on a desk—mine, as it turned out. The yellow curls that were now nothing but a collapsed wig, the eyelashes that looked more than ever like a pair of dead centipedes, and the ridiculous pink dress. That was, for the moment, all that remained of Miss Blossom.

7

The Stupidest Man Alive

"Satisfied?" inquired Miss Switch.

"Well . . . well, why did you have to go and disguise yourself in that loony outfit?" I asked, rising to my own defense. "No . . . no wonder I didn't know who you were."

"Loony?" said Miss Switch.

Oops! I could tell by the tone of her voice that I had made a huge mistake. On a scale of one to ten, it was several million degrees below the temperature of ice. I could practically feel her glass-green stare boring a hole in my lame brain.

Now I have to admit that much as I liked Miss Switch, every time I met up with her as her actual self, it was pretty scary. It always took me a while to get used to the idea of what she was. I mean, when you've spent all your life thinking certain things about certain kinds of people, it's hard to start thinking something else on a moment's notice. So even though I knew I'd be crazy to think good old Miss Switch would ruin my future by turning me into a toad or a bat or a lizard just to prove a point, still, a witch is a witch is a witch. There are certain things in life it pays to bear in mind, and it seems to me that's one of them.

"What I meant to say is 'unusual,' Miss Switch. It's really okay. Actually, not bad at all," I said, backpedaling like crazy. "How did you come up with that . . . er . . . interesting hairdo?"

"That came from a picture in a fashion magazine I found while I was swooping around one night," Miss Switch said. "Of course it wasn't exactly a new magazine."

I was smart enough to keep my mouth shut on this one. "Where did you find it?" was all I asked.

"I happened to float by a house where some people were clearing out their attic. I spotted the magazine, and went floating back for it later. And I found the dress there as well. What a find! Don't you agree?"

"Sure do!" I replied, getting smarter by the minute.

"I designed the eyelashes myself!" Miss Switch said proudly.

"The finishing touch!" I said.

"Of course, I had some trouble with the lip paint," Miss Switch said, giving me a narrowed, sideways look.

"It . . . it looked fine to me," I said.

"Now I *know* you're lying, Rupert!" Miss Switch snapped. "But the point is, does your fertile mind have any ideas as to how to modify the fashion picture?"

This sounded like a question loaded with land mines. I hesitated. Then I hesitated further.

"Oh, come, come, Rupert," said Miss Switch. "I need some help here."

"Well," I said, "how about . . . how about getting rid of some of the frills and bows on the dress." My heart was going a mile a minute as I waited to see how Miss Switch would take this.

Her eyes narrowed further. Her eyebrows raised. Then she dropped down at her desk, picked up a pencil, and started making notes. "Rid of frills and bows," she muttered as she wrote. "Next?"

I was feeling a little bolder. "You might trim the eyelashes," I suggested.

"Trim eyelashes," wrote Miss Switch. "Next?"

"I'd work a little harder on the . . . er . . . lip paint," I said. "Straighten it out a bit."

"Work on lip paint," wrote Miss Switch. "Next?"

"That leaves the wig," I said, and gave a deep sigh. "I'm afraid I don't know what to tell you about that."

"Hopeless?" said Miss Switch.

"Sort of," I replied.

"Hopeless. Do the best you can," wrote Miss Switch. She laid down her pencil with a thump. "Now that's done with, but I can't tell you how good it feels to be back in my own cozy outfit. Even that gray number I wore in the past is better than my latest disguise."

"Then why don't you just go back to it, Miss Switch?" I asked. "The class would sure be glad to have you back."

"Impossible!" said Miss Switch. "I can't blow my cover."

"Miss Switch," I said, "does your cover include letting the class get away with what it's been getting away with?"

"You noticed?" said Miss Switch.

"Who wouldn't?" I said. "And I guess if you have to keep on being Miss Blossom, that's the way it's going to be."

"Afraid so," said Miss Switch. Then her eyes delivered a few more angry sparks. "But if you don't think I'd like to take Billy Swanson's and Melvin Bothwick's heads and knock them together, you have another think coming, Rupert. But I presume you've also noted that some learning was actually going on in the sixth grade, too, despite all?"

"I did notice that, Miss Switch," I replied. "And now that I know Miss Blossom is really you, I guess I'm not surprised."

"Thank you, Rupert," said Miss Switch, giving me her version of a modest smile. "And I'll see what I can do about the spitballs."

"But are you going to tell me why you came back?" I asked. "And why you're . . . er . . . undercover?"

"Yes, yes, of course," said Miss Switch. "Find yourself a desk, Rupert. We have a great deal to talk about."

As my desk was already occupied with the remains of Miss Blossom, I figured I might take Peatmouse's desk. But before I could even make a start for it, something leaped off the teacher's desk and landed right where I was standing. It must have been behind a pile of books, because I hadn't seen it.

"Brow-ow-owl!"

"Woke up from your nap, eh, Bathsheba?" said Miss Switch. "You remember Rupert, don't you? Rupert, you remember Bathsheba, I'm sure?"

"Oh, absolutely!" I said. And I remembered something else, too. A certain party in my jacket pocket. I could feel his little body begin to tremble right through the jacket. I quickly leaned over to pet Bathsheba, something I'd never tried before, and with my free hand stealthily zipped up the pocket containing Fred.

"Nice kitty, kitty, kitty!" I said.

"Brow-ow-owl!" growled Bathsheba. She turned to look up at Miss Switch with a pair of eyes just as slanted and glass-green as those of her owner. "Is he balmy? What's this 'kitty, kitty, kitty' stuff?"

"Don't be rude, cat!" snapped Miss Switch.

The two of them glared at each other with their matching slanting, glass-green eyes. Then, with another low, throaty growl, Bathsheba leaped back onto the teacher's desk, sat down, and calmly started washing her whiskers.

"All right, then, cat!" snapped Miss Switch. She jumped up and, with her long black cape swishing around her ankles, strode over and dropped down into the desk next to me.

"Now, let's get down to business, Rupert," she said. "First of all, I'd like to know what you were

58

doing prowling around here at midnight, if you didn't know who I was?"

"My pets started talking to me again," I replied. "That's a pretty good sign you were back, Miss Switch. Actually, one of my guinea pigs thought Miss Blossom might be you in disguise."

"That would be Guinevere," said Miss Switch. "She's one smart cookie, that guinea pig."

"Well," I said, "even though I couldn't believe Miss Blossom was you, I figured you had to be around *somewhere*. My pets and I all agreed on that. We also agreed that you only come back when you're in trouble . . . or I am. Are you in trouble, Miss Switch?"

"Not that I'm aware of," she replied coolly. "But *you* are, Rupert. Big, *big* trouble! Possibly the whole sixth grade."

"But I've thought about it and thought about it, Miss Switch," I said, "and I haven't been able to come up with a single idea about that. I mean, if you'll excuse me, except having to put up with . . . with Miss Blossom."

"Forget *that!*" said Miss Switch. "Doesn't anything else come to your fertile scientific mind? Nobody else new who has entered your life recently?"

I shrugged and made a face. "Nobody but the person who's our acting principal until Mrs. Grimble gets back. There's nothing dangerous about him that I can tell, except that all the girls and ladies are swooning over him. It's really disgusting. But I have to tell you, he's the handsomest man I've ever seen. I mean, we're talking television, the movies, *anywhere*. You've seen him, haven't you, Miss Switch?"

"Yes, and I agree with you, he's without doubt the handsomest man in the world," replied Miss Switch.

"The universe?" I suggested.

"That, too!" snapped Miss Switch

"On a scale of one to ten, Miss Switch," I said, "where would you say that—"

"Oh, for goodness' sake!" Miss Switch said. "That's enough! Besides, there isn't any scale for that man. He is off-the-charts handsome. But he happens to be off-the-charts some other things as well."

"What?" I asked. Was this man off-the-charts brilliant? Was he off-the-charts famous? My ears were tingling.

"What he is," said Miss Switch, "is the stupidest man who ever lived! He is such a dim bulb, he couldn't find his way out of a cookie jar. He also just *happens* to be Saturna's bonehead brother!"

Saturna! So she *was* mixed up in this somehow, I thought. I *knew* it!

"Saturna has had more trouble dealing with various witches who have made idiots of themselves over him," Miss Switch went on. "She tries to keep him occupied, but it's practically impossible. His broomstick-flying skills are almost nonexistent. He keeps ramming into things, or getting himself rammed into by some passing witch who can't keep her eyes off him. Saturna's put him in charge of a cave near Witch's Mountain, which requires no brains at all. So why she would send him to Pepperdine to do her dirty work for her is beyond me. He's nothing better than a windup toy, and hasn't an original thought in his head. But with Saturna in the wings somehow managing him, I can't take any chances.

"That's why I've come as Miss Blossom, Rupert, and have to put up with spitballs and all the rest even if it ruins my good disposition. But Saturna's got to be running the show somehow or other. If I could just figure out how!"

"Miss Switch, I know!" I blurted excitedly. "I know exactly how!"

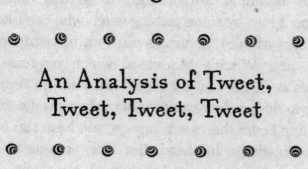

8

An Analysis of Tweet, Tweet, Tweet, Tweet

Having delivered this piece of what I considered to be amazing news, I sat back in Peatmouse's desk and waited for Miss Switch to be suitably amazed.

"What are you babbling about, Rupert?" she inquired. "Just how could you know anything like that?"

"I only figured it out by accident. It's why I needed proof you really were Miss Switch. I thought you might actually be Saturna!" I announced. "I know Saturna has it in for me because I wrecked the computowitch."

"Computowitch! Oh, how I hate the sound of that word! That stupid little machine condemning me to sweep Witch's Mountain for one hundred fifty years if I didn't come up with some original witch-craft!" Miss Switch leaped up from the desk and began to stride furiously up and down at the front of the classroom. Her eyes were shooting out so many sparks, I had to duck to keep from having some of them sizzle right on me.

"I . . . I'm sorry, Miss Switch," I said meekly. "I didn't mean to get you so upset."

Miss Switch flopped back into Creampuff's desk, pulled out a tablet of lined yellow paper from under the lid, and began fanning herself. "No apologies necessary, Rupert," she said. "After all, you're the one who came up with the idea of telling that machine what a popular teacher I was with the Pepperdine fifth grade. That astonishing piece of news completely wrecked it. No more issuing orders. Gone! Never to be heard of again!"

"Not . . . not exactly gone, Miss Switch," I said in a very small voice.

She turned and glared at me. "What do you mean, not exactly?"

"I'm afraid it's sort of . . . sort of come back," I said, cringing.

"WHAT?" howled Miss Switch.

"It's okay, Miss Switch. It really is!" I nearly choked getting this out as fast as I could. After all, I wasn't anxious to have another fireworks display. "It's come back in a different form . . . via a genuine computer! But now that I know about this, I think it's going to be *very* helpful."

"It better be!" moaned Miss Switch.

"It is. I'm sure of it," I said. "I found out about it when I was writing an e-mail to Spook. That's Amelia, who's left town with her family, Miss Switch. I was telling her how I hoped you'd be appearing again. I got around to mentioning the computo-witch, and my computer suddenly went crazy, the screen shivering, colors changing, my computer heaving in and out like it was having trouble breathing. I'm not going to go into the whole thing now, because it's just the end of it that matters. After my computer settled down, it had the word 'computo-witch' on the screen. I was doodling around and added a '.com' to it, and guess what?"

"I gather you hit on a Web site, Rupert," Miss Switch said excitedly. "Go on!"

"You're exactly right, Miss Switch," I said. "But there was nothing on it because I needed a password to get in. I took a stab at it, and guess what again?"

"SATURNA!!!" Miss Switch threw her head back and gave an unearthly howl of glee. It was the kind of howl, I have to confess, that was always a spooky reminder of what Miss Switch was.

Miss Switch rubbed her hands together with a triumphant look on her face. "Saturna's private Web site . . . computowitch.com! Just think of it . . . a direct line to that dim-witted brother of hers, Grodork, aka Mr. Dorking, Pepperdine's beloved principal, and I can find out everything Saturna has to say to him—every one of her instructions!"

"Does . . . does that mean I don't have a thing to worry about?" I asked.

Miss Switch's slanted eyes narrowed to glass-green slivers. "Not at all, Rupert. You're still in danger, and for that matter, so possibly is the whole former fifth, now the sixth grade. After all, *they're* the ones who made it possible for you to put the original computowitch out of order by expressing their . . . er . . . regard for me as a teacher. And Saturna's a very, very clever witch. I may know what she's up to, but then I have to find a way to outwit her. We can take no chances. Now, would you like to report to me what you've read so far on computowitch.com?"

I had to shake my head. "Miss Switch, what she wrote was all in some kind of nutty rhymes. I'll bring it up on my computer as soon as I get home and make a copy. You'll have it first thing tomorrow."

"Not good enough. Time is of the essence," Miss Switch said. "Let me see, hmmmm. Doesn't Pepperdine have a computer or two lying around, Rupert?"

I jumped up. "Sure they do! A whole roomful for computer class, and two of them can connect to the Internet. Probably be safer if we don't turn on any lights, but I've got my flashlight. I'll bet you've never operated a computer, have you, Miss Switch? I'll show you how it works."

"I'm a quick learn," said Miss Switch. "Come on, Rupert, let's do it. You coming with us, cat?"

"I'll pass on this one," Bathsheba said. "After all the excitement, I'd like to just stay here and enjoy the peace and quiet." She started to wash her whiskers again, and before she had finished with the first whisker, Miss Switch and I were on our way down the dark hall, the light from my flashlight bobbing along ahead of us.

Fred was along with us, too, naturally. As we walked down the hall, I unzipped the pocket with my free hand and reached in to give him a reassuring pat on the head. He gave me a reassuring peck right back on my finger. I quickly zipped the pocket back up, and was I glad I did!

"Brow-ow-owl!" Bathsheba came bounding down the hall after us. "Changed my mind," was all she said.

"Your privilege, cat," said Miss Switch

By then we had arrived at the computer room. Miss Switch moved up a chair for Bathsheba, and then leaned over me, watching every move I made. I have to say I felt pretty important demonstrating something to someone who was not only my teacher, but a witch as well. Not to mention her know-it-all cat.

"Okay, Miss Switch," I said. "Now stand back and get ready for the show." I typed in "computo-witch," and sure enough, everything happened just as I expected it would: screen shivering, colors changing, machine heaving in and out.

"You're quite positive the thing isn't going to explode?" asked Miss Switch.

"Absolutely!" I said, now feeling like an old hand at this.

I was right, of course. Everything calmed down. The word "computowitch" arrived back on the screen. I added ".com" and the "enter password" box immediately appeared on the screen.

"Quick! Quick! Enter it, Rupert! Enter it!" Miss Switch drummed excitedly on the back of my chair with her long, bony fingers. "The suspense is killing me!"

"Well, here goes!" I said, and with great deliberation I typed the name "SATURNA."

Wham!

Bang!

The same homepage appeared with all the stars and moons and weird lines around the border. And the very same words!

"There it is, Miss Switch," I said. "Exactly what I got before."

"Be still, Rupert!" Miss Switch said. "Just let me read it." And so while I was reading it on the screen, Miss Switch read it aloud.

> **"How very sweet**
> **Tweet, tweet, tweet, tweet,**
> **I'll have my chance**
> **To howl and dance,**
> **No one's in sight**
> **Except that fright,**
> **No you know who**
> **Is in the brew,**
> **Bats may squeal**
> **And vultures wheel,**
> **But do not fear**
> **The way is clear."**

For a few moments after Miss Switch finished reading, the room was silent. Deadly silent. And then a huge shower of sparks flew over my shoulders at the screen. I held my breath, waiting for the explosion I knew was going to follow. And it did!

Miss Switch gave a blistering howl of rage. "How very sweet, tweet, tweet, tweet, tweet! Who does that creature think she is, a canary? I'll put *her* in a cage someday, and see how much tweeting she does. Have a chance to howl and dance, will she? Oh, not if I have anything to do with it, my pretty. And I suppose the 'No one in sight/Except that fright' refers to Miss Blossom. That's rich from someone whose face would scare the warts off a hog! But she has a head stuffed with moon dust if she thinks 'you know who' is not in the brew. 'You know who' is in the brew, and in the stew, and in the know, Madame Saturna. Oh yes, tomorrow Miss Blossom, aka you know who, aka the fright, aka Miss Switch, rides again!"

Miss Switch really had me all charged up. "Hurrah!" I shouted, waving my fist in the air. "But now you know, Miss Switch, why I wasn't sure Miss Blossom was really you. I mean, how was I to know Saturna hadn't set a big trap for me."

"And she might have, Rupert," Miss Switch said. "Make no mistake about it. She might be making a huge blunder regarding Miss Blossom, but she's still dangerous. We can't let down our guard. We'd be on a very slippery slope if you hadn't discovered computowitch.com."

"I'll check it out first thing in the morning," I

said. "I have to be careful, though. If my parents happen to come around and see my computer carrying on the way it does, they'll run in and pull the plug and not let me near it again until my father has taken it someplace to be looked at. But I'll see what I can do. Of course, we can always use one of these computers when no one's around," I suggested.

"But you'd be in hot soup if anyone just happened to surprise you and walk in." Bathsheba gave a wide yawn and stretched. "Might I be allowed to make a suggestion?"

"Yes! Yes! Yes!" Miss Switch said impatiently. "But be quick about it, cat. I have papers to correct, and Rupert has to get home for his rest."

"Well," Bathsheba drawled, "I noted that Rupert waited for the machine to go into its song-and-dance routine after he typed 'computowitch.' When it was all over, he put in the '.com.'"

"So?" inquired Miss Switch.

"So," said Bathsheba, "why not just type in 'computowitch.com' all at once? Why give those self-important little machines with their puffed-up egos the grand opportunity to show off? Cut them off at the pass, is what I say. Oh well, try it or not, it's your choice."

"It's a waste of time," I said. "It only works one way."

Bathsheba flicked her tail back and forth. "Up to you," she said indifferently.

"The cat may have a point, Rupert," said Miss Switch. "If we don't want to sit through the whole show, we can always pull the plug. Go ahead, do it!"

This sounded more like a command than a request, and I made a point of never arguing with Miss Switch. "Oh, all right," I grumbled. "But I don't think it will work."

I quickly typed in "computowitch.com." Not a second's pause after the word. And in the "enter password" box, I typed "SATURNA."

Wham!

Bang!

There was the same Web site just as it had been before I turned off the computer.

"So there you are!" said Miss Switch.

"Well, what do you know!" I said. "Gee, thanks, Bathsheba! I don't know if I ever would have thought of that."

Anyway, I didn't mind too much losing to a smart cat like Bathsheba, even if she did have a pretty high opinion of herself.

"Don't mention it," she said, and never even lost a beat finishing an ear wash job.

Then I went back to Room Twelve with Miss Switch and Bathsheba because I decided I'd just as soon leave the same way I arrived, through the Room Twelve window.

"Now, Rupert," Miss Switch said as soon as we had entered the room, "please remember that when you return here tomorrow, you will find Miss Blossom and not Miss Switch."

"I got that message," I said.

"If you have anything you wish to report to me, have it in writing stapled behind your homework papers," Miss Switch continued. "Or you may leave a message on my desk. But be certain I'm right there to see it. If we have to confer, it will have to be done *very* carefully. If we're caught with our heads together, that could make even a numskull like Grodork, aka Mr. Dorking, suspicious."

"I'm right with you, Miss Switch," I said. "Is that it?"

"Yes, Rupert," she replied, "except for one other important thing. I have to warn you that whatever you notice happening in class, you'll please keep it to yourself. No eye contact with any of your friends, or with me, either. Is that clear?"

"Sure," I said breezily, not realizing how difficult that assignment might turn out to be.

"Then, run along, Rupert!" Miss Switch motioned me toward the window.

"Boy, Miss Switch," I said, "I can't wait to e-mail Spook . . . er . . . Amelia, and tell her you're back."

"Absolutely not, Rupert!" Miss Switch glared at me. "No such thing."

"Wh . . . Wh . . . Why not?" I stammered, taken aback. "Don't you trust her?"

"Of course I trust Amelia," said Miss Switch. "That's not the point. It's just that I consider it highly dangerous to have all this classified information flying around out there via e-mail."

"Telephone, then?" I suggested hopefully.

"Don't even mention it," she said.

"Spook already knows something is going on," I said. "What if she asks?"

"Punt," said Miss Switch. "Amelia's smart enough to figure out what's what. Take my word for it."

"I suppose I can't even tell my pets," I said, realizing as soon as the words were out of my mouth that one of them was already knee- or, rather, *feather*-deep in this whole situation.

"Don't be silly, Rupert," said Miss Switch. "Of course you can tell your pets. That's an entirely different matter."

"Well, good night, then, Miss Switch," I said, and started to climb out the window. With one leg over the windowsill, I hesitated and looked back. An interesting thought had occurred to me. "Miss Switch," I said, "did *you* ever . . . well . . . swoon over Grodork, aka Mr. Dorking?"

Miss Switch instantly impaled me to the window with her deadly glare. My blood turned to ice. What had I been thinking asking a stupid question like that?

Then, all at once, Miss Switch threw back her head and started howling. With laughter! "Did you get that, cat?" she said.

"I . . . I . . . d-d-did!" replied Bathsheba. She was down on her back, her paws flailing the air, shaking so hard, she could hardly talk. "I've never heard anything so funny in my life. Imagine *you* swooning over that moron. Oh, that's rich, it is!"

"Me mooning over that imbecile!" Miss Switch shrieked. "What a picture!"

"Stop! Stop!" Bathsheba screeched. "I can't stand it!"

The two of them were still screeching and howling, chuckling and chortling and gasping for air as I sneaked away. I felt like a prize idiot.

"Well, that was interesting," Fred said as I unzipped my pocket and lifted him out.

"You don't know the half of it," I said, as I put him back on my shoulder and started for home.

9

Ominous Gobbledygook

To: broomstick@home.com
FROM: spook@home.com
subject: nose under control

what's all the mystery? i'm going crazy waiting to find out. but i'm not going to ask a lot
of questions. i know you used to think i was
pretty nosy, and i was. i am. but as you've found
out, i can keep my nose out of things if i have
to and i have a strange feeling i'm supposed to
now. right? and i won't say any more about what
you told me not to say anything more about.

school here is okay. Not great, just okay. Are you still looking for the **toadstoolius spookus returnicum?** I'm looking here, but I have a feeling you'll have more luck where you are, especially at good old Pepperdine, considering what we found there before. Write when you can, whatever you can.

spook

TO: spook@home.com
FROM: broomstick@home.com
subject: Nose control appreciated

Got your letter and am writing this short one before I leave for school. Just wanted to tell you not to go crazy. Keep cool. And thanks for keeping the nose under control. I'll explain when I can. Please don't give up. The pets send their best.

Broomstick

I hated not writing more to Spook, but I knew if I did, the chances were I'd say too much. I felt I was on safe ground mentioning the pets. After all, animal people often sent regards from Rover, or love from Tabby, in their letters. There was nothing remarkable about my pets sending their best, except I was pretty sure Spook might figure they actually had, which meant they were talking to me, which meant Miss Switch was back. But I knew Miss Switch was right. Spook was smart enough to know what was what, and would say no more about it.

As soon as I'd sent this off to Spook, I was ready to see if there was a new message from Saturna. And was I ever grateful to Bathsheba! This time there was no quivering and heaving in and out, and other weird noises. In absolute silence, the computo-witch.com homepage appeared on the screen. Saturna must have been up early, because there *was* another new message.

> **"Yes, I approve!**
> **You're on the move,**
> **The play's the thing**
> **Revenge to bring,**
> **Come, disaster**
> **Fast and faster,**
> **Begin the coup**
> **And start the stew,**
> **No need to tell**
> **Your surprise spell,**
> **I trust your brain**
> **To be their bane,**
> **And cannot wait**
> **To hear their fate."**

I couldn't wait to hear what Miss Switch had to say about this one. To me it seemed like more of Saturna's gobbledygook, but with some pretty ominous added words thrown in. "Revenge." "Disaster." "Coup." And the word "fate" again. But nowhere did I see anything like instructions being fed to Grodork, aka Mr. Dorking. I was certain, though, that I was missing something and I needed Miss Switch to figure it out. I really would like to have told my pets everything that had happened, but I knew Fred would take care of that. Then I had to get over the hurdle of meeting Peatmouse, Banana, and Creampuff on the monkey bars.

"Boy, how did we ever manage to get a teacher like Miss Blossom?" Creampuff said.

"You'd think this being our last year at Pepperdine, they'd have given us someone decent," Banana said, and gave a big groan.

"Yeah, like Miss Switch," said Peatmouse.

"Yeah," we all agreed.

You can imagine that it was all I could do to keep my mouth shut further on that one. It was also all I could do not to catch Miss Blossom's eye as we filed past her desk to drop off our math homework en route to our own desks.

My homework, of course, had a copy of Saturna's report clipped to the back of it. Miss Blossom gave us all such a big, vacant smile, I couldn't help wondering if she had remembered her request. But I had no sooner dropped into my desk when I saw her draw out my sheet from the pile of homework papers and slide it into a drawer.

No one else noticed this, naturally. It was good old Miss Switch at work, and she had always been very good at doing a lot of things no one in the class noticed. Well, excepting myself. Which is why I saw one of Billy Swanson's spitballs come flying back at him like a pebble from a slingshot and zap him on the cheek. And Melvin Bothwick get his neck frozen sideways when he was trying to stick his nosy nose into someone else's book bag.

"Oh, you poor thing!" Miss Blossom purred to Billy.

"Would you like me to rub your neck for you, dear?" she said to Melvin.

Being called a "poor thing" nearly ruined Billy for the day. And Melvin looked as if he wished himself on another planet at the thought of Miss Blossom massaging his neck in front of the whole sixth grade. Miss Switch was back in the saddle again, and no one (but me) even knew it!

In the meantime, though, I was going batty wondering when I'd be able to consult with her about Saturna's report. Miss Blossom had barely glanced at the paper I'd attached to my math homework before she slid it into her desk drawer. Was I just going to have to make it back to Pepperdine at midnight again?

The day dragged on, with no sign from Miss Blossom. But something else interesting finally did happen in the afternoon. Mr. Dorking showed up in the classroom, along with Miss Tuna and her big notebook. The female population instantly swooned, including Miss Blossom! I nearly fell right out of my desk when I saw her batting her crazy eyelashes at him. For a split second I actually believed her. Then I began thinking of the scene of Miss Switch and Bathsheba howling with laughter in this very room just a few hours earlier. I had to conclude that Miss Switch was not only a witch and a great teacher, but a very clever actress as well. She was batting away at such a rate, I was afraid her fake eyelashes might fall right off!

Mr. Dorking was a man of very few words, probably because he didn't know very many, or how to use what he had, but he hardly needed any. All he had to do was cast his eyes around the room. When he finally did speak, out came golden tones that sent the girls into even further swoons.

His purpose in visiting the sixth-grade classroom, it turned out, was to announce that the first PTA meeting was to be held the following week, and the sixth grade was being invited to put on a scene from a play. He said he had always liked the balcony scene from *Romeo and Juliet,* personally. More swoons from the girls at this, of course. However, he seemed to have difficulty in even getting this small announcement out, and had to refer to Miss Tuna both for the day and the time when the scene was to be performed. I couldn't help wondering how he would manage if the school hadn't had the foresight to get Miss Tuna as his assistant. Anyway, he flashed his big smile at us and left, with Miss Tuna scurrying after him. This was all so fascinating that it wasn't until they had left that I thought of something.

Wham!

Bang!

The words materialized in my head:

The play's the thing
Revenge to bring!

I quickly looked at Miss Blossom. Though it was hard to tell what was going on behind those eyelashes, I was pretty positive that her eyes were narrowed almost to slits as she looked at the disappearing back of Mr. Dorking. That told me she had definitely been in touch with my computowitch.com report, and zeroed in on the same words I had. Saturna had something unpleasant in mind by way of revenge for the sixth grade! The question was what? Miss Blossom and I *had* to talk!

"Well, class," said Miss Blossom, beaming at us, "isn't this going to be fun? Tomorrow we shall begin at once to plan our scene. But our lessons do come first, you know, and I must speak to a few of you about your math homework. Wayne Partlow, Harvey Fanna, and Rupert Brown, will you please stay in the classroom after the closing bell rings? I would like to talk to each of you for just a few minutes."

Now I knew that neither Peatmouse nor Banana exactly sparkled when it came to math, but although my bird, Fred, may have had another opinion, I never really thought I was bad enough to need a conference with my teacher about it. So naturally I knew what this was all about. Miss Switch and I were finally going to talk!

I admit I was getting to be a pretty good actor myself. I just sat at my desk looking cool and exchanging faces with Peatmouse while Banana had his conference up at Miss Blossom's desk. Then, even though my heart was thumping away, I sat and stared out the window with a blank face until they were both done.

"See ya at the monkey bars!" Peatmouse called.

"See ya!" I called back, and sauntered up to Miss Blossom's desk. As soon as I arrived there, she pulled a sheet of paper from the drawer and laid it down on the desk.

"Amazing!" she said peering closely at it. From past experience, I recalled that Miss Switch had often gotten carried away with actually being a teacher instead of a real, honest-to-goodness practicing witch. So could I have actually been called up to her desk to discuss my math homework? I inched closer to her desk to see what she was studying so closely. I was relieved to discover that it *was* my copy of Saturna's report.

"What's amazing about it, Miss Switch?" I asked, tingling with anticipation.

"Miss Blossom! Miss Blossom, Rupert!" she said impatiently. "When I'm in this costume, it's 'Miss Blossom.' We have to keep our focus here. But what's amazing is that a message like this can be plucked out of thin air."

"Not exactly thin air, Miss Blossom," I said. "More like a thin wire."

"Thin air, thin wire, who cares? It's still astonishing," said Miss Blossom. "You don't think science is going to overtake witchcraft, do you, Rupert?"

"Not a chance, Miss Blossom," I replied. "I mean, take getting a broomstick airborne on its own steam, or going back in time, or a person being turned into a lizard or a woolly caterpillar. Never happen."

"In all fairness, Rupert," said Miss Blossom, "we do get help from certain little bewitching aids. You know, eye of newt, wing of bat, tongue of toad, and items of that sort."

"I don't think any of those things would do much to move science forward, Miss Blossom," I said.

"You may be right," said Miss Blossom. "At any rate, what did you conclude from Saturna's message?"

"Nothing much, at first," I replied. "Now it looks as if the class is going to be putting on the play mentioned. But I have to tell you, Miss Blossom, 'revenge' and 'disaster' don't sound too good."

"They don't, indeed! You are dead right about that, Rupert," said Miss Blossom. "But did you conclude anything else?"

"Afraid not," I replied. "I mean, I couldn't detect any instructions you said Saturna was going to be spoon-feeding to Mr. Dorking, so how are we supposed to know what she has in mind for him to do?"

"Bingo!" shouted Miss Blossom. "I knew you'd get it! You're absolutely right, Rupert. There *are* no instructions. Which means, I am sorry to say, that we are in very deep trouble!"

I didn't like the sound of this. "What . . . what kind of trouble?" I asked.

"Rupert," said Miss Blossom, "if Saturna is not issuing instructions to Grodork, it can mean only one thing. It means that for the very first time since I've known him, that brother of Saturna's, from somewhere in the vacant space he has between his ears, has actually come up with an idea of his own!"

"Are you sure?" I asked.

"Of course I'm sure!" replied Miss Blossom grimly. "Analyze it, Rupert. What does 'I approve' suggest to you?"

"I guess that Saturna approves something someone else has done," I replied.

"Exactly!" said Miss Blossom. "Grodork! He has some surprise spell, and Saturna's buying the idea. Blast and botheration! Here I thought we had a direct link to Saturna's brain. Devious it might be, but at least we'd know what we were dealing with. The question is how does Grodork communicate with *her*? Do you suppose she's set him up with his own Web site that she can pick up—dodo.com, password grodork, or something like that?" Miss Blossom smiled thinly at her little joke.

"More likely he just sends her an E-mail," I said.

"Well, if he can do that," said Miss Blossom, "why can't she just communicate with him the same way without all the computowitch Web site nonsense?

"It's the privacy issue, Miss Blossom," I replied.

"I just discovered computowitch.com and the password by dumb luck. But sending an E-mail with the kind of stuff she's sending via a computer to Pepperdine Elementary School would be the height of craziness. All the teachers have E-mail addresses here and anybody can pick them up. blossom@pepperdinees.edu would probably be yours, if you were interested. I think that the school secretary distributes the teacher E-mail a couple of times a day. What would she think if she happened to light on dorking@pepperdinees.edu and read Saturna's poetry?"

"I wouldn't touch that with a ten-foot pole," said Miss Blossom.

"Exactly! But . . . but . . . " I said excitedly, "the messages Mr. Dorking is sending to Saturna could still be in the computer, if he was, well, too stupid to know how to delete them. I could find out right now."

"I can't go with you. Too risky," said Miss Blossom. "But go on! I'll be right here waiting for you."

It was a wasted trip. When I raced back to Miss Blossom in Room Twelve, I had to report that there was nothing.

"No messages from Mr. Dorking to Saturna. Nothing!" I announced. "He's erased everything."

"Blast and botheration!" said Miss Blossom. "Now we're back to square one with nothing but guesswork."

"A play doesn't sound too dangerous, Miss Blossom," I said.

"Don't you be too sure about that, Rupert," she replied.

"Can't you come up with any play-bewitching aids along the lines of eye of newt and that sort of thing?" I asked.

"Oh, there's probably a whole medicine chest full of aids of some sort," said Miss Blossom. "But how would I know which one to use if I don't know what I'm using it for?"

I shrugged. She had a point. "Well, how about toadstools like the kind we used before? Maybe we could locate a *toadstoolius dramaticus correcticum*. Or how about a *toadstoolius shakespearius disastrius preventum?*"

Miss Blossom sighed. "Now you're reaching. Well, maybe not. But there's only one chance in that gazillion you're always mentioning that we'd find them, especially that second one. And I don't know if I'd recognize them if we did. There are no two ways about it, Rupert, we are in very big trouble."

For a few minutes, the classroom was sunk in gloomy silence.

"I guess," I said at last, "what we could use is a fairy godmother."

"WHAT?!!!!!!!!!!"

Oops! Bad idea. I had to duck to avoid being pelted by a tornado of sparks whipping about the room.

"FAIRY GODMOTHER! Don't even mention them to me. We witches get more bad press from just swooping around at Halloween, and generally doing more or less what's expected of us. All up front, all very straightforward. But those devious creatures—why, most of them are worse than we are. They've caused more trouble with those three wishes they offer than you can shake a broomstick at. Why, I could tell you some tales that . . . oh, never mind. They're beneath discussing."

"I'm sorry, Miss Blossom," I said meekly.

"Not your fault, Rupert, just don't believe everything you read about them," she said. "And I must be honest, there are some very decent fairy godmothers. And there are also some very nasty witches, which happens to be what we're involved with now. But I'm afraid we'll have to do the best we can. We'll just have to keep our noses to the ground, our eyes peeled, and our ears pricked, or whatever."

Well, I couldn't think of any "whatever" that would do much good. It was scary. And there was good old Peatmouse waiting for me out on the monkey bars, with no idea at all of the danger that he and I, and the whole sixth grade, might be headed straight for.

10

A Bunch of Eyewash

"I can't figure it out," Peatmouse said as we were sitting out on the Pepperdine monkey bars the following morning. "I think I'm actually learning something. I mean, considering who's our teacher."

"Me too," said Banana. "Anybody here thinks she's maybe as good as . . . well, as good as Miss Switch?"

We all looked at each other and shrugged. "Nobody's *that* good," I said, which I just happened to know was exactly the truth.

"I don't know how she does it when she's such a

mess doing everything else," said Creampuff.

"*Romeo and Juliet*! Lo-o-o-ove! Sheesh!" Peatmouse said.

"Yeah!" we all agreed.

"But that was dorky Mr. Dorking's idea, not Miss Blossom's," Creampuff said. "I guess she had to go along with it."

"Yeah," said Banana. "There're only two people in the balcony scene, though. I wonder what the rest of us will be doing?"

"What do you mean, 'rest of *us*'?" Creampuff said. "What makes you so sure you won't be the lucky one who gets to be Romeo?"

"Not me," Banana said. "I can't do heights. I'll just tell Miss Blossom if I have to climb a ladder to any balcony, I'll throw up all over Juliet."

We all knew this was not exactly a true statement, considering that at that very moment Banana was dangling from the top rung of the monkey bars. But we didn't say anything. After all, we knew we'd all back up any of our excuses no matter what they were.

Of course, of everyone there, of everyone in the whole class, actually, I was the one person who could be sure of not having to be a Shakespearean actor. Miss Blossom would be counting on me to do some very serious detective work, especially at the performance, where she would be busy with the PTA and trying to keep the sixth grade under control. She'd be counting on me to go snooping around, not standing up on a ladder waving my arms. That is, of course, if we ever *got* to that point without discovering what Grodork had in mind for the sixth grade, and having Miss Switch put a stop to it. Yes, indeed, I was quite safe from having to play Romeo, but I would stand by my friends and do all I could to keep it from happening to *them*!

Miss Blossom announced as soon as the bell rang that morning that we would be having tryouts for the scene just before lunch.

"I'm so sorry there are only the two roles," said Miss Blossom, flapping her eyelashes at us and giving us this big sympathetic smile. "I'm sure you all want a part. But the rest of you will be onstage as an audience just as they were in Shakespeare's day. Now, won't that be fun?"

Well, it would be more fun than the alternative, at any rate, I thought to myself. But Miss Blossom was half right when she said we would all want to win a part. All the girls wanted to be Juliet. After all, Mr. Dorking would be out there with the rest of the PTA watching them. But none of the boys cared to be Romeo. And there were all sorts of escape routes tried. As for me, what I did was read the part in such a dead voice, nobody in their right mind would have even cast me as a doorpost. Miss Blossom smiled sweetly through it all.

Jessica Poole got chosen to be Juliet. And guess who got chosen to be her Romeo? I could have dyed my face blue. I could have suddenly grown a tail or ears the size of flapjacks. It wouldn't have made any difference. Miss Blossom had me in mind all along, and the tryouts for the Romeo part were just a bunch of eyewash. I sidled up to her desk as soon as the classroom had cleared for lunch.

"Excuse me, Miss Blossom," I said, "but what's the big idea of making me Romeo? How am I going to keep my nose to the ground, my eyes peeled, and my ears pricked if I can't spend my time lurking around instead of standing on a ladder in front of everyone making an idiot of myself."

"And just exactly where you should be!" said Miss Blossom.

"Excuse me again, Miss Blossom," I said. "But are you referring to the idiot part, by any chance?"

"I don't care to dignify that question with a reply, Rupert," snapped Miss Blossom. "I was, of course, referring to your being in the play, which means being at every rehearsal without having to 'lurk around' to be there. What, pray tell, do you think Mr. Dorking, aka Grodork, even with his limited brain power, will think if he shows up at rehearsals and finds you 'lurking around'?"

"But won't Mr. Dorking get suspicious, anyway, when he gets a load of my acting talents, which don't exist?" I asked. "I mean, considering my connection to—er—Miss Switch?"

"When I think of your performance at Witch's Mountain putting that computowitch out of commission," said Miss Blossom, "I have every confidence you'll do just fine. Get Guinevere to work with you on this. I have a feeling she's a guinea pig with talent as well as brains."

Acting lessons from a guinea pig! This could have been funny under any other circumstances. But the consequences of my blowing this could be serious. It could wreck Miss Switch's Miss Blossom cover if it didn't appear as though I was chosen for the part for my great acting talents. I was going to have to put on a good performance no matter what. I just hoped Guinevere was up to the coaching job. I knew I was going to need all the help I could get!

11

No Clues to Anything

Actually, it wasn't nearly as bad as I thought it was going to be. At first the boys were all calling me "Romeo" just as I figured they would. But when Peatmouse, Banana, and Creampuff reminded them that if anything happened to me one of them might get picked in my place, they quit. All except for Melvin Bothwick, who went on and on about it. Romeo-o-o. Romeo-do-do. Romeo, lay-ee-hoo. He wouldn't let it alone. If you want to know my personal opinion, I think he wanted the part himself. But eventually, when he'd been told enough times by several boys to dry up, or cut it out, or go lay an egg, he finally gave up.

Then, once the flurry of tryouts was over with, even though the scene we were going to do couldn't last more than a few minutes, Miss Blossom somehow managed to keep everyone busy. It was amazing to me how such a small production required so many stage managers, costume consultants, set designers, and people in charge of props, not to mention doing double duty as "the audience" up onstage. Every sixth grader was made to feel that without his or her presence, the performance would be a flop. Of course, I could see the fine hand of Miss Switch behind the whole thing!

She even came up with the idea of having a musical introduction, so three sixth graders were kept occupied taking care of that. We had Harry Clipper on drums, Joanie Marks on the piano, and Billy Swanson on the harmonica. Music aside, it was my belief that this was a setup for Billy to have his mouth occupied so he couldn't take time out to manufacture spitballs.

As for being Romeo, that turned out to be not too bad, either. Jessica Poole, who got the role of Juliet, wasn't Spook, but rehearsals with her were actually kind of fun. On the home front, Guinevere was a good coach, just as Miss Blossom had said she would be. Of course, Caruso's nose got put out of joint at not being asked to do the job, as he fancies himself quite the performer. But it got straightened right out again when Guinevere appointed him to play the role of Juliet. I'm not sure that Shakespeare ever envisioned a turtle in the part, but who am I to say? At any rate, all in all, things were going very smoothly. Except for two problems.

Mr. Dorking's absence was problem number one. "I thought he'd be hovering around every chance he could get," Miss Blossom said. "I haven't seen him around once."

"Heck, Miss Blossom," I said. "If he hasn't been hovering, I could have been lurking instead of being Romeo!"

"I haven't noticed any suffering on your part, Rupert," said Miss Blossom sharply. "You actually seem to be enjoying yourself. Furthermore, Guinevere's efforts appear to be paying off. Your guinea pig should be proud of you, Rupert."

"Thanks, Miss Blossom," I said modestly. "And yes, she is. But do you really think I'm good enough to make Mr. Dorking think I got the part legitimately?"

"Oh, absolutely!" said Miss Blossom. "He won't suspect a thing. That is, if he ever shows up. I'm beginning to get the terrible feeling that it won't be until the actual performance at the PTA meeting.

And we haven't got a single clue as to what's going to happen there. That blasted computowitch.com Web site of Saturna's isn't telling us a thing."

And that, of course, was problem number two.

"So, what do you make of it all?" I asked.

"What I make of it," replied Miss Blossom, "is that Saturna doesn't have to tell her lamebrain brother anything because, amazingly enough, he is managing this on his own. And I now have to believe that whatever he has in mind is going to take place on the very night of the performance. It's the worst possible situation."

"And you still haven't come up with any preventive measures, Miss Blossom?" I asked.

"Not a thing, Rupert," said Miss Blossom. "And unless Mr. Dorking tips his hand in very short order, we are, not to put too fine a point upon it, in a big, fat mess!"

"Oh, murder!" I said.

"Precisely!" replied Miss Blossom.

"You look splendid!" exclaimed Guinevere.

"I look stupid," I said. "You don't have to be nice." I had just returned from examining my image in the bathroom mirror. I was wearing the leotards my mother had dredged up for me from her brief fling with ballet lessons right after I was born. I also had on a cape she had made out of an old gray chenille bedspread, and on my head I wore something that, no matter how I tilted it to make it look cool, still looked like what it was: a red shower cap with a dyed pink ostrich feather stuck in it.

"I'm not just being nice," said Guinevere. "I mean it."

"I wish I could find a pair of leotards for me," Caruso said wistfully. "Think how I'd look in them doing Pagliacci!"

The picture of a turtle in leotards silenced us all for a few moments.

"Caruso, I don't mean to be unkind," said Fred patiently, "but that idea is about on a par with you riding around on Rupert's shoulder in a basket."

"Worse, I expect," said Caruso glumly.

"Never mind, dear," said Guinevere. "You do have a beautiful voice."

"It's just a good thing I don't have to sing for the show tonight," I said.

"Have you had any sign yet of what Mr. Dorking has in store for you?" asked Fred. My pets, of course, had had detailed reports of everything that had been happening at school.

"Not a peep, Fred," I said. "It's going to be bad enough having to stand up there looking like an idiot, no matter how good my acting might be, without being scared stiff that I might evaporate or who knows what right there in front of my parents and the whole PTA."

"Terrible!" said Guinevere. "And Miss Switch hasn't come up with anything?"

"No eye of newt, or wing of bat, or anything else?" Caruso said. Like my other pets, he was as much into witch buzzwords as I was.

"Not a molecule of anything," I replied.

By then I was pulling my jeans and sweatshirt over the leotards. I wouldn't be caught dead walking into the school in that outfit.

"Well, gotta go now, pets," I said.

"We'll be anxious to hear all about it when you get back," said Guinevere.

I hesitated at the door. "*If* I get back," I said.

"You will," said Guinevere.

"Miss Switch has never let you down yet," said Hector.

"Witchcraft can accomplish anything," Caruso chimed in.

I had to shake my head at this. "Not always. Not when it's witchcraft versus witchcraft."

"Well, we all have the greatest confidence Miss Switch will pull you through," said Guinevere. "Now you just go on that stage and break a leg."

Suddenly there was a huge flapping of wings in

Fred's cage. "What do you mean 'break a leg'? Isn't he in enough trouble as it is?"

I had to grin. "It's all right, Fred. We've switched from witch to stage talk. 'Break a leg' is what you say to actors. It's a good luck charm."

"Live and learn," said Fred. "I guess there's more to learn in life than where to put the decimal point. Okay, then, break a leg for me, too!"

"Same from us!" said Hector and Caruso.

"Thanks, pets!" I said.

I knew they were sounding more cheerful than the way they really felt. So was I. I was just glad they couldn't see the goose bumps rising under the leotards every time I thought of what might lie ahead!

12

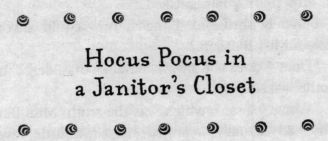

Hocus Pocus in
a Janitor's Closet

The folding chairs in the Pepperdine auditorium were still being set up when we arrived. That's because my mother insisted on being early enough to grab a front-row seat.

Some other sixth graders were gathered where we were all supposed to stay until the business meeting was over, when we were to file out while the parents were having punch and cookies. Miss Blossom was with them, and she caught sight of me.

"Who's that waving to you, Rupert?" my father asked.

"That's Miss Blossom," I said.

"Your . . . your *teacher?*" My mother's eyebrows rose up to meet her hairline.

"That's the one," I said.

"How is it you've never—er—explained her to us, Rupert?" my father asked.

I merely shrugged. I mean, how could anyone explain Miss Blossom?

"Does—does she always look like that, dear?" my mother asked.

"Worse," I said, which was the truth. Miss Blossom had actually *improved* herself a little, even though I knew she couldn't do too much to herself without blowing her cover. Her eyelashes, however, had been clipped a couple of millimeters, and she had another dress that wasn't quite as wild as the first one. The yellow beehive on top of her head unfortunately remained the same.

"I can't quite tell from here," said my mother, "but her dress looks almost as if—as if—well, as if it was something left over from a yard sale."

"Probably was," I said.

"Is she in—in strained circumstances, dear?" my mother asked sympathetically.

"I don't know," I said, "but I do know she helps out a lot of kids."

"How generous!" murmured my mother.

"Maybe we should help her out a little," said my father. "You know, hold a benefit for her or something of that sort."

"I think I'd leave it alone," I said.

Then, before I could be asked to explain that further, I made a hasty departure from my parents.

When I reached Miss Blossom, I raised an eyebrow at her, but she shook her head and hissed under her breath, "Nothing!"

Then Mr. Dorking finally arrived. He came marching down the aisle to seat himself at the table up front with Mrs. Fanna and the other members of the PTA committee. All the ladies present were in a sudden state of swooning. Mrs. Fanna was fluttering to such a degree when he sat down at the table, I thought she'd flutter right out of the auditorium. My mother, of course, was sitting with my father, right in front of Mr. Dorking. I didn't even want to think about *that* situation.

But Mrs. Fanna finally managed to pull herself together and start the meeting. The first thing she did, of course, was introduce our acting principal. Mr. Dorking then stood up and said a few words. A very few words. The fewest possible words he could get away with, because Miss Tuna wasn't sitting up there at the front table to prompt him. But for all it mattered to the ladies in the audience, he could have been up there reciting "Hey Diddle Diddle the Cat and the Fiddle" instead of announcing how happy he was to be at the meeting of the Pepperdine Elementary School PTA. There was a general breeze in the auditorium as all the ladies started fanning themselves with their programs.

I was amazed at how much business finally got conducted despite all this. I couldn't help wondering, though, how things would have gone if it had been known that a witch and a warlock were present, which naturally is not usual for a PTA meeting. Anyway, they got through such matters as fixing the swings, repairing leaky faucets, painting the playground equipment, including the monkey bars, and other things equally fascinating before the meeting ended. The ladies all then clustered around Mr. Dorking as the men made a dive for the punch and cookies.

Miss Blossom quickly herded us behind the stage curtain. I ducked into the janitor's broom closet, removed my jeans and sweatshirt, and threw on my cape and shower cap. I braced myself for the clever remarks I'd get when I reappeared, but there weren't any. Everyone was too busy gulping down cookies and punch in small paper cups that Miss Tuna had delivered to the stage. I was really grateful for the punch, as I needed it to oil my tonsils, which had gone very dry.

Then the sixth-grade make-believe audience climbed onto their make-believe theater benches. Juliet, aka Jessica Poole, climbed up the make-believe balcony, a ladder draped in a sheet painted with green leaves and roses. I, Romeo, aka Rupert P. Brown III, stood surrounded by some artificial potted palms, poised to climb a short ladder in front of it. The orchestra began playing the unrecognizable piece they'd been rehearsing. Then the curtain was pulled.

My heart now began racing a mile a minute as I waited for something terrible to happen. I mean witchcraftwise, not actingwise. Only nothing did. I could see Miss Blossom hovering in the wings, but Mr. Dorking wasn't hovering at all. He was just sitting in the audience with a vacant look on his face, watching the proceedings. It began to look as if Miss Switch and I had guessed all wrong, and nothing was going to happen after all. It was some other play Saturna was talking about. But at that moment, I had to concentrate on being the great actor. The applause died down, and Romeo was up to bat.

I began to speak. "But, soft! What light through yonder window breaks? It is the east, and Juliet is the sun!"

Or at least that's what I thought I was saying. Those were the words I'd rehearsed. Those were the words that had left my brain cells and traveled to my mouth. But what actually came out was the following:

"What's the big deal up there at the window? Is that you, Julie, baby? Come on out. Don't be such a shrinking violet. Let your big hero have a look at you."

Juliet shook her head as if she'd just dreamed what she heard, and needed to wake up. Then she began her speech. "Romeo, Dodeo, where are you, you big wimp! Why don't you tell Daddy where to get off? Go get your name changed, you dummy. I might consider changing mine, but I'd better have something in writing about your great feelings for me. Don't think just swearing is going to do you any good."

By now I was getting a distinct feeling about what was happening. Jessica wasn't, of course, and I saw her clutching the ladder to keep from falling when she heard what was coming out of her mouth. Now, it was clear to me that all this was Saturna at work. But, it somehow didn't relate to those scare words in her so-called poetry. Was this as bad as it was going to get, just making us look ridiculous in front of the PTA? Well, I couldn't stop to consult with Miss Blossom about it, so I just charged on.

"Am I going to have to listen to more of this drivel?" I shouted.

"If you want me, you're going to have to," Juliet

shouted back. "Some things have got to be straightened out. If changing a name does it, then that's what we'll have to do. Personally, I don't care. If you were a cabbage, you'd still smell like a cabbage."

"Hey," I said, "I didn't come here to get insulted. I came here to woo."

"Well, it's my way, or no way. So boo hoo to you," said Juliet.

As we went on trading insults, the sixth-grade "audience" started shouting, and pelting us with crushed paper punch cups and chocolate chip cookies.

"You're no hero, Romeo. You're just a big old dodeo do!"

"You're all wet, Juliet. You'll never snag him—wanna bet?"

"Go get her, Romeo!"

"Go get him, Juliet!"

As Juliet and I ducked the flying paper cups, I could see that things were getting seriously out of hand. I didn't dare look out into the PTA audience to see what *they* were thinking, especially my parents in the front row. I did look for Miss Blossom, but she had disappeared from her position in the wings. I couldn't believe she would just leave her sixth grade to go for a little flight on her broomstick around the block, but where *was* she?

Then suddenly, there was Miss Blossom determinedly pulling on the curtain cords. As the curtains closed, everybody onstage froze for a few seconds. Then they all came back to life, and stared at one another, and shrugged. Nobody really knew what had happened to them. At the same time, we could hear Miss Blossom's voice on the other side of the curtain.

"Well, members of the PTA," she said in a voice ringing with good cheer and enthusiasm, "the sixth grade hopes you've enjoyed their little original surprise this evening. They know it isn't exactly what Shakespeare had in mind for his balcony scene, but they had lots of fun with it, and hope you did, too. Thank you."

The PTA was probably too stunned at first to do much but sit there glassy-eyed. Then two or three parents started to clap, and finally they all began to clap. I guess I would have to say they just about brought the house down. Later, when everyone was milling around, I heard comments such as, "very humorous," "pretty clever," "really contemporary."

Mr. Dorking, though, stood looking as if he didn't know what had hit him. While milling around with everyone else, I managed to break away from my parents and mill myself over to Miss Blossom.

"May I have a word with you, Miss Blossom?" I

asked. "I know this isn't the time or the place, but I have a homework question."

"Any time or place is the right time or place when it concerns homework, Rupert," said Miss Blossom, smiling sweetly. We put several yards between the nearest PTA members and ourselves.

"What do you make of the whole thing, Miss Blossom?" I asked under my breath.

"What I make of it, Rupert," she replied, "is that dimwit Dorking couldn't come up with anything better than the twisted tongue bewitchment. I knew it the moment the first words came out of your mouth. It's one of the simplest bewitchments going. He cast a spell on the punch served to the class."

"But it didn't taste any different to me, Miss Blossom," I said. "Just plain old grape."

"Don't be ridiculous, Rupert," said Miss Blossom. "You can't taste a spell. Well, perhaps in strawberry, but never in grape. But, fortunately, I had with me a few of your basic emergency anti-bewitching aids, and while you were onstage, I dipped into the janitor's closet to perform the appropriate hocus-pocus."

"So that's where you were!" I said. "But how did you manage to—um—unbewitch all of us the moment the curtain was closed?"

"Nothing to it," replied Miss Blossom. "All I had

to do was sprinkle . . . but we haven't time to go into that here, Rupert. I just want to warn you that I don't believe this is what Saturna had in mind for you and the sixth grade. She must have had a mental lapse when she agreed to any surprise spell from that dumbbell Dorking. Well, she'll be surprised all right when he tells her what actually happened."

"What if he doesn't tell her?" I asked.

"Oh, he'll tell her, all right," said Miss Blossom. "He'll have to."

"Why?" I asked.

"Vibrations," replied Miss Blossom. "Or witch's vibes, as we call them. How do you suppose I knew you might be in the kind of trouble where my expertise was needed? Vibrations, Rupert, vibrations! Saturna's vibrations will tell her that her brother fell on his handsome face, so he might as well confess what happened."

"Well, what are we going to do about it, Miss Blossom?" I asked.

"Check computowitch.com," replied Miss Blossom grimly. "I'm coming back here later tonight to pay a visit to the computer room myself. Then we'll both be checking it. We'll compare notes tomorrow. But I expect that at midnight tonight, when Saturna learns how that lamebrained brother of hers has fallen on his gorgeous nose, the fur will fly. She'll be furious—and even more dangerous!"

I didn't like the sound of this at all. I had been hoping the worst was over, but it looked as if it was just beginning! At that moment, though, I did have another minor problem on my mind. "Miss Blossom," I said, "what am I going to say to my parents about what happened tonight? What are any of the sixth graders going to say to their parents?"

"No need to say anything," replied Miss Blossom. "By the time everyone leaves Pepperdine tonight, no one but you, and of course Pepperdine's beloved principal, will remember that anything out of the ordinary went on. The sixth grade will think everything happened just as they rehearsed it, and the parents will believe that's what they saw. It's all part of the anti-bewitchment package. Now, you'd better run along—and get a good night's sleep. You have to be ready for your math test tomorrow."

Math test! Now just how was I supposed to be thinking about a math test when I knew a furious Saturna was still out there dangerous and armed with witchcraft!

13

Not Your Usual Mode
of Transportation

Naturally, as soon as I arrived home, got rid of the leotards, and reported to the pets all that had happened, I turned on my computer. But computo-witch.com still had the same old stuff on it. Miss Blossom was right. There probably wouldn't be anything until midnight. After all, Saturna might well have been vibrating away up there on Witch's Mountain, but until she got the specifics from Grodork, there wouldn't be much to hurl back at him.

As I suspected, it was almost impossible keeping

my mind on grammar homework and studying for a math test with everything else I had on my mind. I was also pretty wiped out from being Romeo and the other evening's events. But every time my head started to droop, I felt a sharp peck on my cheek. Good old Fred knew I wanted to stay awake long enough to try computowitch.com again at midnight.

Midnight finally arrived, and I didn't lose any time in turning my computer back on. Unfortunately, only half of my brain was awake, the wrong half. I typed in the word "computowitch" as usual, but then stopped to sleepily, and I might say leisurely, scratch an itch on my ankle. Before the other half of my brain came to and I realized what I was doing, it was too late. The computer had already started in on its old routine. Pea-green quivering screen. One color change after another. Computer heaving in and out.

I have to hand it to Fred. He didn't flutter a feather, but sat on my shoulder watching this all happen.

"I goofed, Fred," I said.

"Don't worry," he said. "It didn't crash before. It won't crash now."

"I know," I said. "I'm not too worried. But it's just sort of stupid, that's all."

Well, of course we were wrong. I guess my computer had finally had it with all this quivering and heaving in and out. It just upped and crashed right before my eyes. Gone. Finished. So no computo-witch.com that night. Nothing to turn in to Miss Blossom with homework the next morning. I'd just have to wait for a report from her. I don't have to tell you, I was pretty disgusted with myself.

Miss Blossom found out at once, of course, that there was nothing attached to my homework. She didn't find out why, though, until the lunch break. She had asked if someone would kindly stay behind a few minutes when the lunch bell rang to help her with something, and my hand shot up so fast I almost dislocated my shoulder. At least I saved anybody else from having to volunteer. But it was then, after I'd told her that my computer had crashed, that I found out Miss Blossom hadn't reached com-putowitch.com, either.

"But I did learn something very interesting instead, Rupert," she said. "Hold on to your hat. This is going to knock your socks off!"

I didn't bother to let Miss Blossom know she had mixed things up a little there, as I was learning more and more about keeping my mouth shut when there's nothing to be gained by opening it. But what Miss Blossom had to say really did knock my socks off.

"The door to the computer room was shut when I came back at midnight," she began. "But there was

114

a pale light coming from under it. I suspected it must be Grodork making his report to Saturna. Needless to say, I did not risk opening the door to peek in. Bathsheba and I simply hid behind the doorway of the room across the hall. We waited and we waited. I began thinking someone might have gone off and left a light on in there. Then I heard voices, those of a man and a woman. There was no mistaking Grodork's, but I couldn't guess the other. And then I heard Grodork addressing the owner of the voice by name, Neptuna!"

"Neptuna?" I said. "Who the heck is Neptuna?"

"Well you may ask, Rupert," replied Miss Blossom. "I confess it gave me pause for a moment. But I believe she is no other than Mr. Dorking's shadow . . . Miss Tuna!"

"Do you mean we have *another* witch here at Pepperdine?" I croaked.

"It does look that way," said Miss Blossom.

"How . . . how come you didn't recognize her before?" I asked.

"Because I've never seen her before," Miss Blossom said.

"Not even a photograph?" I asked.

"Rupert," said Miss Blossom, "you may have seen a painting of someone's idea of a witch, or you may have seen a drawing of same. You may have even seen pictures of people dressed as witches. But have you ever seen a photograph of a *real* witch?"

I had to shake my head. "No."

"And you never will," said Miss Blossom. "We don't register on film. Like it or not, that's the way it is."

"Did you actually *see* her?" I asked. "Are you sure about this?"

"I didn't actually see her, not coming out of the computer room, at any rate," replied Miss Blossom. "But it stands to reason and makes this whole thing fall into place. You see I'd heard through the grapevine that Saturna had taken on an assistant who doesn't look like much, but whose brain is as big as Saturna's brother's is small. There's been a problem with Neptuna, however. She is apparently so ga-ga over Grodork that she's been stupid about that man from the moment she laid eyes on him.

"Saturna has had nothing to worry about, however, because Neptuna could have been a piece of straw from some old broomstick for all the attention Grodork paid her. So Saturna must have come up with the perfect revenge on me at last—send the two of them to Pepperdine. Neptuna as the brains . . . Grodork as the handsome cover. So it's Neptuna we've been dealing with, which explains how that so-called poetry of Saturna's has been deciphered. But this is bad news."

"Come to think of it, Miss Blossom, it was Miss Tuna who served us our punch tonight!" I blurted.

"Exactly!" said Miss Blossom.

"But she can't be all that smart if the best she could come up with was that twisted tongue spell," I said.

"Hmmmph!" sniffed Miss Blossom. "I have a feeling that was Grodork's idea, and she went along with it because around him her brain turns to mush. Anyway, I couldn't wait long enough last night to find out what Saturna had to say. I'm sure she was planning an earful for the two of them, which is why it took so long. I waited until daybreak, and then decided to depend on hearing from you in the morning."

"Boy, I'm really sorry I let you down, Miss Blossom," I said.

"Nothing to do with you," she said. "It's just that blasted computowitch nonsense. But no matter. We'll simply meet here tonight and see what Saturna has to say for herself."

"W-W-We?" I stammered. I have to be honest. I didn't relish those late-night trips on my own to Pepperdine.

"Of course, *we*," Miss Blossom said briskly. "I need your support and expertise, Rupert. I'll be picking you up about a quarter till midnight."

"P-P-Picking me up? In what, Miss Blossom?" I guess I was still pretty groggy from the night before.

Miss Blossom sighed. "Pull yourself together, Rupert. Have you never heard of a broomstick?"

Broomstick! Of course! What had I been thinking? I nodded sheepishly.

"Have you a problem with any of this, Rupert?" Miss Switch asked.

"No problem at all!" I replied. Problem? Was she kidding? I was already imagining myself climbing aboard and zooming off into the night behind Miss Switch.

"You can wipe that look off your face, Rupert," she said sharply. "We're not going on a picnic. This is deadly serious. I only wish we didn't have to wait until midnight. Who knows what might happen this very afternoon. Saturna will not wait very long for a repeat engagement. You may mark my words!"

Well, I did mark them, and she was right. We did get that afternoon off, so to speak, but we got an announcement about something that was to happen the next day. It came via a long note to Room Twelve delivered by Miss Tuna from Mr. Dorking. Miss Blossom read it to us.

It seemed that the school had been lucky enough to be able to get passes to special exhibits at the museum. There were just enough passes for the sixth grade, and we were going the very next morning. Somehow, it sounded fishy to me. Just how fishy it might actually be, though, I wouldn't know until midnight that night. Midnight, and the museum trip the very next morning! Just how much time did that give Miss Switch to do anything about it?

14

Toadstools at Midnight

It was a long wait until midnight. Since I didn't have my computer to tinker with, I just fooled around with a couple of unsuccessful experiments I'd been working on after I'd finished my homework. And, of course, I talked things over with the pets. They were very excited about Miss Switch picking me up by broomstick. She had done it before, but it had all happened so quickly, they hadn't even seen her. I promised them I'd delay climbing aboard a few minutes so they could at least catch a glimpse of her through the window. But they were also pretty anxious about the trip to the museum.

"Look," I said, "I shouldn't have made you all upset about this. What could go wrong on a silly little trip to a museum?"

"*You* said it sounded fishy," said Hector.

"I shouldn't have," I said. "What do I know?"

"Well, we must all remember that Miss Switch will be with them," said Guinevere. "If there's any problem, she'll know what to do about it."

"Maybe not," said Caruso. "You remember what Rupert said about witchcraft versus witchcraft."

"Look here," I said, "we haven't even seen the next word from Saturna. There may not be any problem at all."

"I wish you'd take me along, Rupert, just in case," Fred piped up.

"See here, Fred," I said, "we went through this before. What exactly could you do if there's a problem? What could any bird do?"

"You never know," he replied. "Take canaries. Miners used to carry them along into the mines to sniff out dangerous gases."

"I don't think there are any dangerous gases in a museum," I said. "Besides, you'd have to go in my pocket. I know you were there before, but that was for about an hour. This would be for three hours, at least. How would you like *that,* Fred?"

"If it was the same pocket with the hole in it for breathing purposes, I wouldn't mind," he said. "And I'd pack a lunch. It would be an interesting experience."

"Three hours is a long time. What if you needed to—er—poop?" I asked.

"I'm a big boy now," Fred replied. "I'd take care of that before I left. You wouldn't have a thing to worry about. I'd really like to go."

"Well, I'll think about it," I said. "But don't count on it. Anyway, I'd better get ready. It's about time for Miss Switch to show up."

I'd barely thrown my jacket on and stuffed my trusty flashlight into a pocket when there was a knock on my window, and Miss Switch was hovering outside it. Then I remembered I was supposed to drag my feet just a little so the pets would have a chance to see her. But I had a better idea. I opened the window and stuck my head through before starting to climb out. It was only about nine hours since I'd seen her as Miss Blossom, so I really had to pull myself together seeing her out there hanging in midair on her broomstick in her flowing black cape and tall, pointed black hat. But I was happy to see that Bathsheba wasn't with her for what I had in mind.

"Miss Switch," I said, "would you consider stopping in my room for a couple of minutes to meet my pets? It would mean a lot to them."

"Oh, absolutely!"

Almost before I realized what was happening, she was climbing through the window. The broomstick was in park, and just hung outside the window, not going anywhere. "Miss Switch," I said, pointing as I gave out each name, "may I introduce Guinevere, Hector, Caruso, and Fred. Pets, this is Miss Switch."

"How do you do," said Miss Switch.

"H-H-How do you do, your . . . your royal witchness!" Caruso said, and promptly fell right over on his back. I knew, of course, that he'd been trying to do a stage bow, but he never seemed to learn that a turtle couldn't do that. I didn't say anything but just went over and turned him right side up.

"'Miss Switch' will do just fine," she said at once.

"How do you do, Miss Switch," said Guinevere.

"P-P-Pleased to meet you, Miss Switch," quavered Hector.

"M-M-Me, too," added Fred in a trembling chirp.

"Well, it's a real pleasure to meet all of *you*," said Miss Switch. "I've heard a great deal about you. Rupert is really fortunate to have such good friends."

I stood there speechless. I'd never heard Miss Switch—that is, as Miss Switch and not as Miss

Blossom—ooze so much charm. The pets were frozen with awe, but she had them thawed in no time. In a very few moments, they were all chattering away at warp speed.

"I wish we could offer you some refreshments, Miss Switch," Guinevere said finally. "I mean, something besides guinea pig feed and birdseed."

"Why, that sounds delicious," Miss Switch said without even blinking. "But I've stayed much longer than I should, and Rupert and I must be on our way."

As the pets all knew the importance of what Miss Switch and I had to do, there was no arguing with this. "Good-byes" had to be said. I waved to them as I climbed through the window after Miss Switch. As soon as I was settled on the broomstick, we took off, heading straight for Pepperdine.

I have to tell you there's nothing in the world like this mode of transportation. It was as great as I remembered it. And, of course, I'd never flown to school before. I couldn't help wondering when we arrived at the Pepperdine playground what Peatmouse, Banana, and Creampuff would have thought if they'd been sitting on the monkey bars and seen me zooming overhead on a broomstick toward the Room Twelve window. At any rate, we climbed through and made our way to the computer room. Bathsheba was sitting there waiting for us.

"The coast is still clear, but you were gone long enough. What kept you?" Bathsheba growled.

"I went in for a few minutes to meet Rupert's pets," Miss Switch replied. "For your information, Bathsheba, they all have exquisite manners. You could learn something from them."

"Introduce me!" said Bathsheba, coolly flicking at her whiskers.

"Yes, and watch you pick bird feathers out of your teeth for a week!" said Miss Switch. "Now, let's get on with this, Rupert. Who's going to do the honors?"

"Carry on, Miss Switch," I said.

She did, and then we just sat there staring at the screen together as Saturna's new message appeared. It was very long. It was no wonder Mr. Dorking and Miss Tuna had to sit there half the night waiting for her to compose it.

"Oh, gnawing rats
And stinging gnats,
Oh, brimstone boil
And poisons roil,
Oh, witch's brain
Sunk down the drain,
To trust the school
To such a fool.
How all was hung

On twisted tongue
I can but guess,
But nonetheless
I can guess well
How came the spell.
But one mistake
Is all you'll make,
Or what you'll get
You won't forget.
But not too late
To seal their fate,
No you know who
To spoil the stew,
But I want clear
They disappear.
My shrinking trick
Is what will stick.
You have the stuff
But just enough
To work one spell,
So do it well.
The field trip fling
Is just the thing,
And, oh, what joy
To get that boy.
Revenge at last,
Oh, what a blast!"

"Boy, you sure were right about the twisted tongue thing, Miss Switch," I said.

"There was never any doubt about it, Rupert," she replied. "But that's been and gone. What we have to think about is what's to come. Saturna seems to have given Neptuna and Grodork the ingredients for the shrinking bewitchment, her specialty. I suspect they were to use it to begin with, but he got giddy with his own powers and we know what happened with that. As for the field trip, I have no doubt that refers to our visit to the museum tomorrow."

"I knew it sounded fishy," I said, "coming up all of a sudden like that. But this time around, Miss Switch, we don't just know where and when, we know *what*. I sure don't like the sound of shrinking. You can have all your anti-bewitchment stuff ready, can't you?"

"Of course I can!" snapped Miss Switch. "However, Rupert, I must tell you we may know where, when, and what, but there is still one big problem. We don't know *how*. Her shrinking bewitchment requires a medium. It could be anything, and a trip to the museum doesn't suggest a single one to me."

"Maybe they'll serve us grape punch when we get there?" I suggested hopefully.

Miss Switch's response to this was a glassy-green stare with a couple of sparks thrown in for good measure. "No, Rupert," she said at last. "If the truth be known, we're not much better off than we were with the twisted tongue. There is, however, one difference. I will have with me the anti-bewitchment formula. It will only be useful if I can discover where to use it. But at any rate, I won't have to leap into a janitor's closet to perform any last-minute hocus pocus."

"Where *will* you be leaping, Miss Switch?" I asked.

"Into Room Twelve, and right now, Rupert. We haven't time to lose. This particular anti-bewitchment formula takes a few hours to mellow. And I'm going to need your help." Miss Switch jumped up from her chair, turned on the flashlight, turned off the computer, and strode to the door. "Come along, Rupert. Come along, cat!"

"Brow-ow-owl!" Bathsheba leaped after her, and I came scurrying along behind.

"M-M-My help, Miss Switch?" I stammered. I mean, what did I actually know about spells, and anti-bewitching formulas? Actually, nothing. "Wh-Wh-What am I going to be doing?"

Miss Switch waited until we had entered Room Twelve before replying. "I have here with me the vital elements needed for the formula: wart of toad, three hairs of hog, claw of vulture, and tail of lizard, along with the more common elements of wing of bat, and your eye of newt. However, I'm still missing one very important ingredient. And that's where you come in, Rupert."

As she was talking, Miss Switch was pulling out the Bunsen burner, a flask, a measuring cup, and a small empty bottle with an eyedropper in it, all from the class science supply cupboard. Then I had to keep on waiting for my instructions as she lit the Bunsen burner and filled the measuring cup with a little water from the class sink.

"What I want you to do, Rupert," she said, "is to take your flashlight, go out to the playground, and bring me a few toadstools."

Now, I'd been out hunting toadstools in the past for Miss Switch. In the Pepperdine playground. At midnight. Alone. I have to admit I didn't enjoy the experience.

"Did . . . did you have any special variety in mind, Miss Switch?" I asked nervously.

"Why yes, I did, Rupert," she replied briskly. "It's the *toadstoolius enlargius instantium.*"

"Gee whiz, Miss Switch, how am I supposed to know one when I see it?" I complained.

"It's a common variety, Rupert. Just scoop up a

bunch of toadstools, and I assure you there will be several among them. I'll have everything else ready when you return. Don't forget to take along a paper sack from the art cupboard."

Anyway, there I was in the Pepperdine playground. At midnight. Alone. And I didn't care any more for the experience than I had the first time. But the thing was that midnight seemed to be a very good time for toadstools. I harvested a bunch of them and when I got back, Miss Switch was busy adding the last of crumbled hairs of hog to the measuring cup. I handed her the paper sack. She emptied it at once onto her desk and began sorting through the toadstools with her long fingers.

"Ah," she said, "just as I expected, several excellent specimens of *toadstoolius enlargius instantium*. But what have we here?" She picked up two toadstools and examined them closely. "Hmmm, these are rare finds, indeed. The Pepperdine playground never ceases to amaze me. Nothing I can use right now, but I am getting some strong vibrations indicating that I may be able to use these very toadstools soon."

"What are they, Miss Switch?" I asked as she shoved them into a pocket.

"Not now, Rupert, not now. This spell requires concentration," she said, crumbling one of the remaining toadstools into the measuring cup. Then she started mumbling to herself as she picked up the glass rod. "Pour into flask. Shake, don't stir. Place over Bunsen burner. Don't begin spell until five bubbles rise."

As soon as this had all happened, she began swooping and swooshing around, waving her arms over the flask. Then she began to moan the words,

"Higglety pigglety, oh, what, slop
The shrinking game you have to stop.
Snakes and spiders, fleas and flies
Bring them back to their right size.
Ricketty, racketty, hullabalooly
Or face the wrath of yours truly."

I have to be honest. This didn't sound a lot better than the poetry Saturna was dispensing via computo-witch.com. Still, a spell is a spell, and if it does what it's supposed to, who am I to comment on it? All in all, Miss Switch put on quite a performance. I might even have been scared if I hadn't seen her do something like it before.

When it all ended, the liquid in the flask had boiled down to practically nothing, just enough to fill the small bottle with the eyedropper.

"Is that enough?" I asked.

"It's powerful stuff, Rupert," Miss Switch replied. "A tiny drop is all that is needed for this particular unbewitchment. If only I knew exactly where I'm going to have to use it!"

Well, we had done all we could do. We cleaned up Room Twelve, and then Miss Switch flew me home.

The pets were waiting up for me. I really didn't want to tell them the whole story of my trip to Pepperdine because I knew it would worry them. But I've always been honest with my pets, so I didn't hold anything back. Besides, what if I returned as, say, a lizard, or a beetle, or didn't return at all? They had to be prepared. At any rate, I have to say that nobody went to bed very happy that night.

15

The Shrinkage Solution

It was really nice out the next day, considering what might be about to happen on our field trip. The note from Mr. Dorking had instructed us to go directly to the bus that would be waiting for us at the Pepperdine front door. It was already there when I arrived, and Miss Blossom was standing at the front door, checking each of us off as we climbed aboard. I could tell that her sharp eyes were checking us *out* as well. And I knew just what she was looking for. Clues to Saturna's medium. Or the medium itself.

"Nothing!" she hissed to me as I climbed past her onto the bus. "We're flying blind again."

I tried doing a little sleuthing myself, looking over the rest of the sixth grade as it filed by. I didn't do any better than Miss Switch. No surprise.

When we arrived at the museum, Miss Blossom stood at the door again as we trooped out, handing us our tickets. There were actually two special exhibits going on at the time. One had to do with Egypt. One had to do with outer space. Our tickets would be punched at the Egypt exhibit, and then again when we entered outer space.

"And you had better guard them with your life, dears," said Miss Blossom. "Otherwise you will be cooling your heels in the lobby."

I don't know if I thought I was going to be pickpocketed or something, but I personally clutched my ticket all the way into the museum before I finally thrust it into a jacket pocket . . . the jacket pocket with the hole in it. It was not a brilliant move on my part, although it was a very small hole and probably wouldn't have made any difference, anyway. As it turned out, it was a good thing I hadn't given my pocket choice too much thought.

Now, I have to mention here that my jacket pockets are rarely empty. They almost always contain such items as candy wrappers, pencil stubs, a couple of paper clips, an interesting pebble or two, a few remains of some cheese crackers. And so on. But one thing I had never found in a pocket was a bunch of feathers. Wrapped around something warm. Something warm that moved. I quickly dropped down on one knee and pretended to tie my shoe.

"Fred?" I hissed. "Fred, what are you doing here?"

"I came with you," Fred replied, sounding a little nervous.

"Well, I can see that!" I said. "But I don't recall telling you that you could."

"No, you just said you'd think about it," chirped Fred. "You never said any more about it, so I just made a command decision. After what you told us last night, I wasn't going to let you go without being around to watch over you."

"But what you did was downright dangerous," I said. "What if someone like Billy Swanson had bumped into my pocket? You'd have ended up bird-burger, Fred. Well, you're here, and I can't do anything about it now. Did you remember to pack a lunch?"

"I didn't need to," Fred replied. "You've got enough cracker crumbs in here to sink a canoe."

"Well, I appreciate your concern, Fred," I said. "But you really shouldn't have come."

"Miss Blossom, Rupert's talking to his shoe-laces," I heard Melvin Bothwick, class snoop, report-ing.

"Are you all right, Rupert?" Miss Blossom asked at once.

"Just broke a shoelace," I said, jumping up. "Sorry about the delay."

Oh, my aching eyebrow! Now I had a stowaway I had to worry about, as if I didn't have enough on my mind. But as we wandered the halls of the museum, waiting to enter the exhibit, nothing seemed to be happening. No shrinkage. No nothing. I looked over at Miss Blossom, threw out my hands, and shrugged. But I could see her eyes darting up and down and everywhere. The class trip wasn't over yet.

Then it was time for our turn in the Egypt exhibit, so we got our tickets punched, got handed a pam-phlet about what we were going to see, and trooped in. I stuck my ticket back in the same pocket because I wanted to give Fred a pat on the head. Then I just wandered around with the rest of the class looking at ancient cracked pots and pieces of pots and other such thrilling items. Nobody was too interested in ancient Egypt, but we had to stay there until our time for outer space. There was still nothing unusual hap-pening by way of shrinkage. When I looked at my reflection in a window, I couldn't see my head getting any smaller or anything like that.

Then Miss Blossom sidled up to me. "Rupert, tell me something," she said. "Don't you usually come just about up to my chin?"

"I think so, Miss Blossom," I replied.

"Well, where do you come up to now?" she asked.

"Your—your shoulder?" I stammered.

"Exactly!" she said. "It has started, and I still haven't found the medium. You were fine outside the exhibit. I checked. So it couldn't be the tickets I handed you. That crossed my mind."

"Are you thinking the pamphlets we were all given?" I asked. "Isn't that pretty far-fetched?"

"It is, Rupert," replied Miss Blossom. "But it's the only thing we have. I want you to come with me and distract each person while I administer a drop of the anti-bewitchment formula to his or her pamphlet. If I'm right about this, you'll be back up to my chin before we get to the second sixth grader. You remember—*toadstoolius enlargius instantium!* Come along! We haven't a moment to lose!"

Fortunately, the room was dark enough that what we had to do wasn't too difficult. I'd point out a display window to someone. Miss Blossom would put a drop from her bottle on the pamphlet they were holding. That was it. Nothing to it. There was only one problem. When we finished the whole class, I had now shrunk to an inch *below* Miss Blossom's shoulder!

Of course, the rest of the class was shrinking, too. Nobody knew it, though. It was dark for one thing, but the main reason was that *everyone* was shrinking so slowly and all at the same time, so naturally nobody felt any smaller than they ever had. Actually, even if we all had been wandering the halls of the museum and shrinking, nobody else would have noticed either. After all, there were dozens of groups of students of all ages there. Everyone would have thought we were the Pepperdine fifth grade. Or fourth grade. Or third grade. Or less, as we kept shrinking. To what?

"Miss Blossom, it isn't working! Just . . . just how far *can* we shrink?" I asked.

"You don't want to know, Rupert," Miss Blossom said grimly. "But things are getting desperate. I must think of something!"

And it was then that I felt someone pecking at me through the hole in my pocket.

"Not now, Fred," I said. "We're in big trouble out here."

"What's that, Rupert?" Miss Blossom asked. "You

weren't speaking to your shoelaces again, were you?"

"No, Miss Blossom," I said. "It's Fred. He stowed away in my pocket. I didn't even know it until we got here."

"That's unfortunate," she said, "because he's probably going to shrink away with the rest of you."

"No probably about it!" Fred said. "Look, you've got to listen to me, Rupert. After you put that ticket in your pocket, it was quite a while before you took it out again. All that time, I didn't feel a thing. Then you pulled out the ticket, and when you put it back in your pocket again, there was a hole in it, so I figured someone had punched it. And that's exactly when I started getting smaller. Your pocket, which is a pretty tight fit, was suddenly getting roomier. Then it began to get a lot roomier. Your pocket might have been shrinking, but *I* was shrinking faster. I felt I'd be the size of a hummingbird in no time. I didn't want to bother you, but then I heard the conversation between you and Miss Blossom, and I knew I had to act."

"And right you were to do so, Fred!" exclaimed Miss Blossom, addressing my pocket. "The hole in the ticket! That must be it! The punching of the ticket activated the bewitchment spell! Quickly, Rupert, let me have your ticket!"

I retrieved it from my pocket and handed it to her.

She put a drop of the anti-bewitchment formula on it and handed it back to me. It sure was *instantium*. I shot up to her chin height faster than I could blink!

"I say it once again, Rupert, you have pets of the highest intellect. I must thank you, Fred!" said Miss Switch.

"My pleasure, Miss Blossom!" chirped Fred. "And I might add I'm now feeling much more myself."

"Come along, Rupert," Miss Blossom said, "we must proceed at once."

"What is it you want me to do this time, Miss Blossom?" I asked. "Do you want me to distract everyone while you pick their pockets?"

"Not at all, Rupert," she replied. "I'll just tell each of my students I need to check to make sure they have their tickets, and they are properly punched. What I want of you is to help round up anyone who might have wandered off."

I stayed with Miss Blossom to see the first anti-bewitchments take place. Nobody questioned Miss Blossom's asking to see their tickets. They just handed them right over. Then I had the best example of the hand being faster than the eye that I'd ever witnessed when she put the drop of anti-bewitchment formula on the tickets. It was amazing! Nobody even seemed to notice their change in size. Maybe it was because the room was so dark, or maybe they didn't want to say anything because it would sound a bit loony. Like me talking to my shoelaces. You had to be careful about things like that in the sixth grade.

There turned out to be only one problem. A person was missing. You might have guessed it would be Billy Swanson. So I had to go looking for him, although I had some mixed feelings about this. The class might be improved if Billy Swanson and Melvin Bothwick both shrunk away to zero. On the other hand, they'd been around from the beginning, and we'd probably miss them. I found Billy standing and staring at a display of ancient Egyptian paper. Paper! Billy couldn't stay away from it. Anyway, I decided I'd make it easier on Miss Blossom, who was still busy with everyone else, and take her Billy's ticket. Then I'd return it to him.

"Billy," I said, "Miss Blossom needs to check all our tickets. So please hand yours over."

"I can't," said Billy.

"You'd better," I said.

Billy pulled half a ticket from his pocket and handed it to me.

"Where's the rest, Billy?" I asked.

Billy shuffled around a bit, and then with a sheepish look, handed me a couple of chewed-up bits of pink ticket. Billy couldn't resist. He had made himself some spitballs! He really was a serious spitballaholic. But my big worry then was how Miss Blossom was going to do any anti-bewitchment on a half a ticket and a bunch of spitballs.

However, Miss Blossom never even flinched when she saw what I handed her. She just put on a couple of extra drops of the formula. I handed the whole lot back to Billy, and watched him shoot up to his regular size. He was still so deep into the ancient Egyptian paper display, I don't think he even noticed.

One thing I couldn't understand was why Miss Blossom didn't do any shrinking, considering that she was walking around with a punched ticket in her own pocket. I managed to slip her the question after Billy had been taken care of.

"Bewitchments do not affect other witches," she explained. "Well, except in one or two very, very rare cases. This isn't one of them."

And a good thing, too, I thought. Of course, how was I to know that before everything was over with, I was going to learn just what one of those rare cases was!

At any rate, the entire sixth grade was back up to size by the time we headed for outer space. I was able to enjoy it thoroughly because I knew that whatever was going to happen that day had now happened. It was actually a very neat field trip. The only people who wouldn't think so would be Mr. Dorking and Miss Tuna when they saw the unshrunk sixth grade arriving back at Pepperdine.

I didn't know what I was going to do with Fred the rest of the day, but as soon as we got back to school, Miss Blossom sent me on a round trip home with him. I think she would have pinned a medal on him if she could have.

When I dropped Fred off in my room, I told the pets I was really mad at him. I also told them he was a hero and had probably saved my life. Fred was okay with that.

But Miss Blossom informed me that we had another midnight session at Pepperdine. I wasn't surprised. I didn't think Saturna was through with us. Not by a long shot!

16

Midnight Rendezvous

Miss Switch flew by for me shortly after midnight. Bathsheba was with her, so she didn't come in. She just waved to the pets as I grabbed my flashlight, climbed through the window, and boarded the broomstick. Then we took off.

"I swung by Pepperdine on my way here," Miss Switch said. "No surprise to me that there was a dim light on in the computer room. I had no doubt who was in there, but I swooped down to have a closer look, anyway. Just then, the light went off, so I knew they were leaving. It's so bright out, being only a day away from full moon, I couldn't risk being seen, so I made a hasty departure."

"Do you think they *are* through already because they began much earlier?" I asked.

"Not likely," replied Miss Switch. "You must know by now, Rupert, that midnight is when we conduct most of our business."

"Then that must mean Saturna sent a pretty short message," I suggested.

"That would by my guess," said Miss Switch.

As soon as we had all climbed through the window of Room Twelve, the three of us made our way down the dark hall to the computer room, which was dark as well. It was a good thing Miss Switch had seen the light there earlier as she flew by, as now we could be fairly confident that Mr. Dorking and Miss Tuna had come and gone. Miss Switch lost no time in bringing up computowitch.com, and we'd been right. Saturna's message was very short, and certainly right to the point.

> **"Could you know who**
> **Be in the stew?**
> **It's very late,**
> **We must not wait.**
> **You must be near**
> **My plans to hear.**

Be at my lair,
I'll meet you there
At full of moon
The witch's noon."

"Sounds pretty clear to me," I said. "Saturna's getting suspicious."

"And who can blame her?" said Miss Switch. "Two bewitchments flopping like that. Looks bad on her record, too. And the thing is, the bewitchments *themselves* weren't bad, especially considering that handsome dimwit was part of the act. Saturna may be realizing that there could be some outside influences at work. I'm not surprised she's becoming suspicious."

"Wouldn't you think she'd give up now?" I asked hopefully.

"Wishful thinking, Rupert," Miss Switch replied. "But the really bad news is that we're not going to be given any free hints from computowitch.com, at least not this time."

"So what do we do, Miss Switch?" I asked.

"Not we, I, Rupert," she said. "I'll be making a little trip to Witch's Mountain . . . to Saturna's lair."

"You . . . you mean you're just going to drop in on them?" I stammered.

"Don't be ridiculous, Rupert. She happens to

have this interesting little opening in the roof of her cave. Skylight, she calls it. I'll just park up there and listen in. Furthermore, I might have the golden opportunity to . . ." Miss Switch's eyes narrowed.

"To what, Miss Switch?" I asked.

"Never mind, Rupert," she replied. "It's a long shot. I don't care to talk about it."

"Wouldn't . . . wouldn't you like company?" I asked. "I mean, you might need some help, Miss Switch. It's not like I've never been there before. And I was pretty useful the last time, if you recall."

"All right, Rupert," she agreed at last. "You can ride along."

"Thanks, Miss Switch," I said. "When do we leave?"

"At full of moon, of course," she replied. "Tomorrow night."

"Is witch's noon what I think it is, Miss Switch?" I asked.

"Naturally," she replied, "midnight, what else?"

"Will you have to take along any . . . um . . . witch's aids?" I asked.

"Oh, absolutely!" Miss Switch said. "Just in case."

"You mean in case of the golden opportunity, Miss Switch?" I asked.

"Precisely!" she replied.

"There's one more thing, Miss Switch," I said. "You don't suppose we could, well, pick Spook up and take her with us, do you? She'd go batty if she ever found out I'd been back to Witch's Mountain without her."

Miss Switch rubbed her chin again. "What do you think, cat?"

"I think definitely why not," replied Bathsheba. "I really like good old Amelia."

"All right, then, that's settled," said Miss Switch. "You know how to get to her house, I presume, Rupert?"

"Not by broomstick, Miss Switch," I had to admit.

"You *do* know her address, don't you?" inquired Miss Switch.

"Oh, sure!" I said.

"Then we'll find it," said Miss Switch.

"But shouldn't we let Spook know we're coming?" I asked. "We can't just show up outside her window. I could send her an e-mail."

"On *what,* Rupert?" inquired Miss Switch.

I hadn't thought about that. My computer was still out of order, and using a school computer was not the cleverest idea.

"I'll borrow my father's! And I'll be careful," I

said. "No key words to give Saturna any ideas . . .
um . . . just in case."

"All right, then. Do it!" she said. "But, Rupert,
please remember to tell Amelia not to forget to bring
her earmuffs!"

17

Together at Last!

The next day really dragged. Twice when Miss Blossom asked me a question, I didn't even hear her. She reminded me, sweetly of course, that if I didn't pay attention I'd be warming my desk in Room Twelve the rest of my life. There were times when I wished Miss Blossom would forget that she was a teacher, and keep her mind on being a witch.

I had sneaked down to my father's home office in the basement when I got home the night before to e-mail Spook. As promised, I was very careful about what I wrote. I was also careful to delete the letter as soon as I'd sent it, so that my father wouldn't find it.

TO: spook@home.com
FROM: broomstick@home.com
subject: Your availability for midnight
        phenomenon

will you be at home and free tonight? if you
are still awake at midnight, take a look out
your window. a certain phenomenon will be occur-
ring there that will interest you. i suggest you
have your earmuffs handy. a reply is necessary
soonest. but send it to the above e-mail
address, not mine. my computer has crashed.

broomstick

I sneaked back down to the basement before I left
for school in the morning, and already had a reply.

TO: broomstick@home.com
FROM: spook@home.com
subject: message understood—earmuffs
        ready

got your message. i'll be at my window studying the phenomenon you wrote about. i'll have
handy the equipment you recommended. sounds
exciting. can't wait.

spook

Now all I had to do was make it through the day. Of course, I had to have a talk with the pets about where I was going, and why. I pointed out to Fred that, hero though he was, I didn't want to put my hand in my pocket on this trip and find something warm and feathery in there.

The minutes crawled by that evening, but at last midnight came. It was a sensational night for a broomstick flight. A gazillion stars twinkled. The moon dangled from the sky like a big silver Christmas ball. It was too bad we weren't just going sailing on a broomstick cruise instead of on a trip to Witch's Mountain, with who knew what at the other end. But I tried not to think about that.

The hands on my desk clock hit twelve exactly when Miss Switch arrived at my window with Bathsheba. I knew she had a lot on her mind, but she still managed to smile and wave to my pets through the window before I climbed onto the broomstick. Then we zoomed off into the night.

Spook's house was dark when we got there, except for one upstairs window where we saw the beam from a flashlight. Miss Switch circled the house, anyway, just to be sure there was no one else up. When we stopped at her window, Spook was right there waiting for us. She waved her earmuffs at us as we glided up to the window.

It was quite a reunion. I don't know whether Spook was happier to see Miss Switch, or Miss Switch to see her. Of course, with Miss Switch you have to know what to look for when it comes to showing feelings like that. Also, I might have been mistaken, but I actually thought I heard Bathsheba purring. As for Spook and yours truly, I guess you'd have to say we were pretty pleased to see each other, too.

Spook really was excited. "I want to hear *everything!*" she said.

"Climb on then, Amelia," said Miss Switch. "Rupert can tell you *'everything'* on the way."

I moved back on the broomstick, closer to Bathsheba, so Spook could get on ahead of me. I didn't want to have a busted neck trying to talk to her over my shoulder. There was a lot to tell, and even though I was racing through it, I had just barely finished when suddenly I realized the cruise weather had ended.

The air rushing past us was now icy cold, and we had to put on our earmuffs. The night had grown darker, too; there wasn't a twinkling star in sight. Mist began to swirl around us. We could still see the moon, but it had become a cold, menacing ball of ice. Spook began to shiver, and so did I. We were both tense, barely breathing, as the dark, silent, deadly Witch's Mountain rose ahead of us.

I thought for a moment Miss Switch was going to zoom into it. But she knew right where she was headed. It was toward a kind of add-on tunnel jutting out about halfway up the mountain. As we drew close to it, I could see that there were three broomsticks parked in front of the entrance. But Miss Switch flew right past them and landed our broomstick behind a rock a little farther up the mountain. We all climbed off, and she motioned to us to follow her.

Moments later we had reached an opening at the top of the tunnel. I guessed it was the skylight Miss Switch had told me about. She put a finger to her lips, then kneeled down and peered cautiously through the opening, motioning us to do the same. Saturna and Grodork were down there in their long black witch and warlock outfits, of course. But Miss Tuna was there as well. Miss Switch had figured *that* one right!

Then Saturna started to speak. Her needle-sharp voice carried up the skylight to us. "So now, here we are. I can't believe what has happened. I thought, Neptuna, when I sent you and your great brain to that blasted school with Grodork as your cover, you'd be able to accomplish something. But you're no more than a lovesick idiot whose brains have turned to porridge. Allowing him to talk you into his *brilliant* twisted tongue bewitchment! I wanted the sixth grade and that *boy* gone, but all you did was give them a good time. And my great shrinking bewitchment's gone down the drain. Now what, I ask you, now what?"

"But . . . but," stammered Neptuna, "I *did* get the bewitchments right. Even if one didn't please you, they did go just the way they were designed to go. I don't know why they ended up going backward."

"Well, all I can think is that you must have done something wrong," snapped Saturna. "Added some ingredient that wasn't intended. You did use a clean pot for the shrinking bewitchment, didn't you?"

"Oh, yes!" cried Neptuna.

"It almost sounds as if someone was around to perform an unbewitchment," Saturna snarled. "You're absolutely *certain* that hag Sabbatina Switch wasn't around anywhere? She couldn't be masquerading as that ridiculous Miss Blossom you told me about, could she?"

Grodork finally came to life. "*Nobody* would look like that if they didn't have to."

"But don't think it's all over yet," Saturna said. "I have another bewitchment worked out. It's almost foolproof. I called you here because the instructions are complicated and I have to give you the necessary ingredients. Now come over here to my supply cupboard, Neptuna, while I explain it to you. I don't know what good it will do, but you can listen in if you wish, Grodork."

The three of them walked over to an enormous black cupboard farther back in the tunnel, aka Saturna's lair. Her voice could no longer be heard clearly through the skylight. A bewitchment that we couldn't hear, and would never get over computo-witch.com. This was bad news.

We couldn't hear anything by eavesdropping at the skylight, at least nothing that gave any clues as to what Saturna was planning for the sixth grade, and of course, *me*. After they had finished their business, Saturna, Grodork, and Neptuna returned to within earshot. Then Saturna ushered them to the front door, told them to get back to Pepperdine ASAP, and warned Neptuna that she'd better get things right this time.

"Aren't you coming with us?" Grodork asked.

"What on earth for?" snapped Saturna. "You don't need me to help you find your way back, do you?"

"N-N-N-No," quavered Neptuna. "We can manage."

"Well, I hope you can also manage to get the next bewitchment right and not botch one of the best ones I have. I'm fed up with the two of you," snarled Saturna.

This was all looking pretty bad to me. One of Saturna's best bewitchments, and we had no idea what it was. But to my surprise there was a thin smile materializing on Miss Switch's face.

"Perfect!" she muttered to herself. "She's not going with them. Just what I'd hoped. My golden opportunity!"

I could see from her wide eyes that Spook had heard this, too. But we just exchanged glances and shrugged. Miss Switch had a plan, and we could only hope it worked. After all, we knew that even witches made boo-boo's. This had better not be one of Miss Switch's finest!

"Quick!" Miss Switch hissed at us. "Back to the broomstick!"

We crept hurriedly back to the place behind the rock where the broomstick was parked. Peering over the rock, we saw Grodork and Neptuna take off on their broomsticks. But Miss Switch waited a few more moments.

"I want to be sure Saturna isn't standing there doing anything cozy like waving them off," she informed us. Then she said that she wanted me sitting directly behind her on the ride back. No explanations. We all climbed on the broomstick. She put it in full throttle, and we zoomed off behind Grodork and Neptuna.

Now, this is something everyone probably knows, but I feel I should remind you that a broomstick in flight makes absolutely no sound at all. And, of course, broomsticks don't come equipped with rearview mirrors. So as neither Grodork nor Neptuna had any reason to suspect someone was pursuing them, they weren't bothering to look behind themselves.

"And Grodork is flying behind Neptuna . . . perfect!" said Miss Switch. "It's just as I thought it would be. She has to lead *him,* otherwise he'd probably get lost. But now, Rupert, I'm going to have to give all my attention to maneuvering the broomstick, so I'll need your help."

"I . . . I'll do whatever I can," I said. "Give it to me, Miss Switch."

"All right, then," she replied. "What I'm going to do now is circle around and cross right over close behind Grodork's back. *Very* close. His brain is so overworked following Neptuna, he'll never notice."

"Where do I fit in?" I asked nervously. Was Miss Switch going to have me climb on Grodork's broomstick and wrestle him off it? Was Miss Switch forgetting I was just a skinny, eleven-year-old kid?

But Miss Switch had something else in mind. "Where you fit in, Rupert, has to do with this little bottle," she replied, pulling it from her pocket. "As soon as I approach Grodork, I'll pull out the stopper and hand you the bottle. When his back is right next to you, you're to reach out and pour the contents of the bottle on him. Do you think you can manage that?"

"I . . . I guess so," I said.

"But one thing I must warn you about, Rupert," she replied. "Don't get a single drop on yourself or Amelia. Be very careful!"

"What could happen if I did?" I asked.

"You don't want to know, Rupert. Just *do* it!" Miss Switch ordered.

I have to say that this reply was not too calming on the nerves. Was it too late to get out of it?

But Miss Switch had already begun to describe a wide circle, and was pulling the stopper from the bottle and heading right for Grodork. I felt the bottle being thrust into my hand, and then there we were, right next to Grodork's back! Grodork the warlock, mind you . . . not Mr. Dorking, Pepperdine's beloved principal! My hand was shaking, but I managed to reach out and empty the whole bottle on him. Miss Switch was right, as usual. He never even turned his head as we streaked away. Furthermore, I didn't get a drop on Spook or me, which was a very good thing, as I came to find out. Poison might have been preferable to what could have happened to us.

"What shall I do with the bottle, Miss Switch?" I asked as we circled around again and came up behind Grodork. I certainly didn't want to hang on to it if a remaining drop might spill on Spook or me.

"Toss it, Rupert," Miss Switch replied. "And watch, look, and listen. Something should be happening right about . . . *now!*"

The words had no sooner blown past our ears and into the night air, than we heard Grodork calling out.

"Neptuna! Neptuna!"

"You called?" Neptuna shouted back.

"I did! Oh, you dearest, darling, beautiful creature!" cried Grodork.

"Were you . . . you weren't by any chance referring to *me*, were you?" shouted Neptuna.

"I was! I *am!*" moaned Grodork.

Neptuna did such an immediate about-turn that if she'd been in a car you would have heard the tires squeal. It's a wonder she didn't see us hovering in the background, but her eyes were too glued on Grodork to see anything else. She did another turn and ended up flying right beside him.

"When did all this happen?" she asked breathlessly.

"I don't know," he replied. "I was just zipping along behind you when all of a sudden it struck me that I can't live without you."

"M-M-Me? *Really?*" Neptuna asked. Her broomstick was wobbling so badly, I was certain she was going to fall off.

"Yes, *you*, my precious!" groaned Grodork. "You must come away with me now to my place. There, my pet, we will live happily forever and ever and ever and—"

"But . . . but what about Pepperdine?" Neptuna interrupted. "And what about Saturna?"

"Oh, poop on Pepperdine!" said Grodork. "And poop on Saturna! She can find someone else to do her work for her. Why should we care when we have each other? Just think, my lovely, you'll be mine to look after forever and ever and ever and—"

"I . . . I rather thought I'd be looking after *you*," Neptuna interrupted again.

"Well, that too," said Grodork. "I was hoping you might mention it. Oh, but how I wish we were on the same broomstick together at this very moment. You wouldn't like to climb aboard mine, would you, my lovely?"

"I would, you gorgeous man!" Neptuna exclaimed rapturously. "But what would I do with *my* broomstick? We'll need it, won't we?"

"I hadn't thought of that," replied the gorgeous man.

"And . . . and who's going to tell Saturna?" asked Neptuna.

"She'll find out from someone or other," replied Grodork. "But come, my sweet, let us sail off into the sunset now, together."

"That's the moon, Grodork, dear," said Neptuna.

"Why, so it is," he replied.

And so the two lovebirds flew off into the sunset. Or moonset. Or whatever.

"Will they live happily ever after, Miss Switch?" I asked.

"I certainly hope so," she replied. "I'm not one to hold a grudge. The bewitchment I performed on Grodork is an extremely powerful one, and almost impossible to unbewitch. Neptuna, of course, was bewitched on her own and didn't need any help."

"Could you explain how it all happened, Miss Switch?" Spook asked.

"As soon as I find a place to park, I'll explain," said Miss Switch.

"How about the monkey bars at Pepperdine, Miss Switch?" I suggested, trying to be funny.

"Hmmm," was all she replied.

"Bathsheba, it was a good one tonight, wasn't it?" she said. Then she threw back her head and howled at the moon with laughter.

"Brow-ow-owl!" Bathsheba howled right along with her.

Well, as I've often said, a witch is a witch is a witch, and that's the way they do things. Take my word for it!

18

Anything Is Possible

I never thought I'd find myself sitting on top of the monkey bars in the Pepperdine Elementary School playground in the middle of the night. But there I was with Spook, Bathsheba—and Miss Switch! She had actually taken me up on my suggestion. I couldn't believe it when that's where she finally landed the broomstick. Spook was pretty thrilled about it, being back at her old school. But it certainly gave me a curious feeling. I mean, let's face it, Miss Switch, Bathsheba, and Spook were not exactly Peatmouse, Banana, and Creampuff!

"All right, then," Miss Switch said as soon as we'd settled ourselves. "Where would you like me to begin?"

"Well, I'd like to know what that stuff was that you had me put on Grodork," I said.

"Do you remember the night I sent you out to find me a *toadstoolius enlargius instantium?*" Miss Switch replied.

I nodded. I wouldn't forget *that* night for a while.

"And do you remember," Miss Switch continued, "there were two other specimens in your collection that I thought were rare finds, from which I was getting some strong vibrations?"

"Witch's vibes . . . I sure do remember that, Miss Switch," I said. "Were those the toadstools you took with you to Witch's Mountain tonight?"

"The very ones!" replied Miss Switch. "I put them in an elixir, of course. They were, to be precise, of the genus *toadstoolius potionus amorius perpetuum.* My vibrations were right on target, as it turned out. Not knowing the details of Saturna's bewitchment could have been disastrous. If she'd accompanied Grodork and Neptuna, I don't know how we could have pulled off our stunt. As it was, I was absolutely certain that unlikely pair would never get back to Pepperdine."

"But, pardon me, Miss Switch," I said, "why did you have to go to Witch's Mountain to dump some of this *toadstoolius potionus amorius perpetuum* elixir on Grodork? Why couldn't you have just done the same thing here at Pepperdine?"

At this, Bathsheba's tail bristled. "Bro-ow-owl! Are you dippy, or what?" she snorted.

"No need to be rude, cat!" snapped Miss Switch. "That's a perfectly understandable question. The first person the bewitchee sets their eyes on after the elixir has been applied is the one who is going to be the object of their affection. Here at Pepperdine, that object could have been just about anyone . . . including *me*. It probably *would* have been me unless I was unbelievably nimble. And I can't even imagine what it would be like having that handsome basket case draped around my neck the rest of my life!"

"Is this one of those rare bewitchments you mentioned at the museum that actually works with witches?" I asked.

"Rupert," said Miss Switch, "it works on just about anything that breathes! It's a very sensitive bewitchment, and extraordinarily difficult, if not impossible, to undo."

"I think I can see now why you didn't want any of that . . . that stuff to get on Spook and me," I said.

"Wouldn't all the lovey-doveyness that happened to Grodork and Neptuna have happened to us? I mean, we're only eleven, Miss Switch. Ugh!"

"Ulch!" said Spook.

"You're quite right about what might have happened, Rupert, which is why I issued the warning. You did as you were told, and now you don't have to worry about the subject for several years."

Never, as far as I was concerned. Spook, too, I suspected.

"Do you think Saturna is going to try again?" I asked.

Miss Switch's eyes narrowed. Then they sent out a huge shower of sparks. Some of them went sailing across the Pepperdine playground, but several of them landed sizzling on the monkey bars. "She'd better not! But I don't think you need to worry. I think she'll figure out someday that I must have been around somewhere, and she'll have to get up mighty early on a witch's morning ever to try anything like that again. Now, any more questions?"

"I do have one more," I said. "What about computowitch.com? Do you think Saturna will keep on using it?"

"Not if I have anything to say about it," Miss Switch replied. "You know, I rather fancy it for myself. I certainly intend to see what I can do about taking it over!"

After that, we had no more questions, so there was nothing left but to fly Spook home. It was pretty hard saying good-bye to her when we dropped her off at her window. It was for me, anyhow. I think it was for Miss Switch and Bathsheba as well, even though neither one would admit it. But Spook and I knew there might never be another chance for an adventure like the one we'd just had.

"I know you have to go, Miss Switch," I said as she dropped me off at my window. "But are you coming back to Pepperdine tomorrow?"

"You don't think I'd leave without telling my class, do you?" she snapped. Snapping was okay. I knew she was never happy about leaving.

But my spirits were pretty low at that moment. Mr. Dorking and Miss Tuna had flown off into the sunset. Or moonset, as it was in this case. All that was happening to me was my having to say good-bye to Spook that night, and probably to Miss Switch the next day.

At least I still had my pets to talk to. But I knew that would end, too, when Miss Switch had gone. Or would it? This was the third time she'd been back and my pets had been able to talk to me. Wasn't three times usually a charm? Maybe this time they'd keep right on talking even after she'd gone.

The next morning on the monkey bars, I brought up the subject of Miss Blossom to my friends. "I wonder if she's going to stay," I said.

"Why wouldn't she?" Peatmouse asked.

I shrugged. "Oh, I don't know. I guess because nobody else has."

"I . . . I kind of hope she does," Creampuff said, looking at us sideways to see how the rest of us would take this. "I'm kind of getting used to her."

"She's a pretty good teacher," said Banana. "And I kind of like her, too, I guess."

"But she still isn't Miss Switch," said Peatmouse.

"Yeah," we all agreed.

"Hey!" Banana was running a finger over the top bar. "What are these black spots? They've never been here before."

"Look like burn marks to me," Peatmouse said. "Somebody must have had a fire going someplace."

"Or maybe shooting off fireworks," said Creampuff.

"Maybe," was all I said. After all, there was no point in offering further suggestions. But I was glad those burn marks were there. What few proofs I ever had of my adventures with Miss Switch were shaky at best, or seemed to disappear entirely.

Of course, wouldn't you know, as I looked out

the windows of Room Twelve later that morning, there were the painters out painting the playground equipment, including the monkey bars, just as promised by our good old PTA. So much for that!

As for the rest of the day, it went just like any other school day. Except for the paint job, nothing else happened. But word quickly got around that Mr. Dorking had left, and so had Miss Tuna.

"Maybe they eloped together, yuck, yuck, yuck!" someone said.

"That'll be the day!" said someone else.

Naturally, I kept my mouth shut.

What surprised me was that, other than the above comments and a few others along those lines, nobody seemed to care much, not even the girls. But at the end of the day, just as I expected, Miss Blossom announced that she, too, would be leaving. Then I was surprised again when the whole class moaned at the news. A couple of people even had to wipe their eyes. Well, I guess I really wasn't that surprised, knowing who Miss Blossom really was.

I kept hoping all day that she would have a special message for me. I finally decided that she just couldn't find a way to get me aside, so I resolved to hang around until everyone had left after the final bell. But right after she made her announcement, she handed back our math tests, waved to us at the door, and walked out. Just like that! The class applauded, and I applauded right along with them even though I really felt let down.

I was pretty glum as I walked home that day. Miss Blossom hadn't even given me the chance to thank her for saving my skin. My mind was wandering, and I wasn't paying much attention to my feet, so I went and tripped. Just what I needed—my school papers flying all over the sidewalk. Of course, my math test was with them. I hadn't even bothered to look at my grade. I carelessly turned to the last page to see what it was. Then I shook my head and looked again.

There was a big, red A plus at the bottom of the page, but there was something else, too. It was a message written in black ink in spidery handwriting.

Remember always to stay online
Don't forget
computowitch.com
will someday be mine!
M. S.

I read it. And read it again. Then I leaped up. Who knew when it would happen, but Miss Switch was letting me know that someday I'd be able to get a message from her! I couldn't get home fast enough to report this to my pets!

"Guess what?" I shouted as I burst into my room.

But I was already too late. They all just looked at me with their bright, beady eyes and never said a word. It seemed my three-times-a-charm theory was a big bust. Had I just been imagining all along that they'd been talking to me?

And what proofs did I have that any of the things that had happened to me had actually happened? As I said, the scorch marks on the monkey bars, courtesy of Miss Switch, were now gone—painted away by the PTA. As for the note on my arithmetic paper, that had started to disappear almost immediately, and by nightfall was gone. That figured. Miss Switch wouldn't have wanted somebody casting their unauthorized eyes on a message like that. So I was left with nothing but a small scrape on my windowsill where her broomstick rubbed. Some proof!

Now there was nobody I could even talk anything over with—travel by broomstick, a trip to Witch's Mountain, how we actually had two witches and a warlock in residence at Pepperdine Elementary School at the very same time, or even who Miss Blossom really was. Oh, I could go on writing to Spook, but as I said before, it wasn't the same as having her right there.

When I crawled into bed that night, I just lay

there with my eyes wide open staring at a shaft of moonlight coming through my window, thinking about Miss Switch arriving at that window in the very same moonlight, and wondering if it would ever happen again. I had no idea how much time had passed when I heard a rustling in Fred's cage.

Fred was usually a pretty sound sleeper. Once he'd started yawning and put himself to bed, I never even heard a peep or a flutter from his cage until morning, except for the couple of times he'd taken it upon himself to be my guardian angel. I never even bothered to close the door to his cage because the door to my own room was always closed at night. So what was going on now?

The next thing I knew, Fred was flying from his cage. My room was pretty much flooded with moonlight, so I could see him fluttering across the room like a small, dark shadow.

Just as he had done the night he and Guinevere, Hector, and Caruso had had their quarrel and ended up good friends, he flew over and perched on the side of Caruso's bowl. Then he gave a soft cheep and flew over to land right in front of Hector's and Guinevere's cages. He stood there for a few moments, his head tilted, and cheeped again. After that, he fluttered up, circled around, and started right for me! I snapped my eyes shut. A moment later, I felt him land right on my blanket, hop over to my shoulder, and give me a tiny peck on my cheek! I waited until I'd heard him flutter away before I opened my eyes to see him hop back into his cage and settle himself down for the rest of the night.

Once again Fred had come to my aid and made me realize what a lamebrain I'd been. Just because my pets could no longer talk to me didn't mean I couldn't talk to them, or that they wouldn't understand what I said. I knew I could go right on talking to my pets, and muttering over my homework and my computer every night with Fred perched on my shoulder, taking it all in.

Of course, I intended to go on looking for a *toadstoolius spookus returnicum*. I had concluded, however, that toadstools of the type I'd been dealing with via Miss Switch, or *any* toadstools, rarely appeared in the Pepperdine Elementary School playground in the daytime. Considering the generally unsavory nature of your run-of-the-mill toadstools, this was probably just as well. But I knew I'd have to steel myself to go toadstool hunting at midnight if I ever wanted to find anything useful. I wondered how Fred would feel about going along with me in my pocket. I'd have to ask him.

And who knew what other interesting toadstool specimens I might find—*toadstoolius billius swansonius spitballius terminatium,* for example. Or a homework aid such as *toadstoolius mathematicus incorrectus nomorum.* The possibilities were endless. And assuming I could ever figure out which was which, I could become a veritable toadstool expert.

And then I began to think of the question that Miss Switch had asked me, if I thought there was a remote possibility science might overtake witchcraft. Not a chance, I had replied. But who knew what genus of toadstools I might find that would bring the magic of science closer to the magic of witchcraft?

Take, for instance, the toadstool that would allow you to elevate a broomstick and fly it—no engine, no propeller, no kidding—*toadstoolius broomstickus nomotorus airborneum.* Or how about a toadstool that would help put me in touch with Miss Switch anytime I wanted—*toadstoolius computowitch dottus commus miss switchius websitum.* Those two would certainly be witch's aids that would make Miss Switch's eyes pop!

You might ask if I ever expected to actually find any of these things. Well, I had no idea. All I knew was that I intended to scour the Pepperdine Elementary School playground (even at midnight, if that's what it took), and never give up trying. And I did know something else. It was that first thing in the morning, I, Rupert P. Brown III, great and dedicated scientist, a firm believer that just about anything is possible, would have a long talk about all of this with my pets. Who else?